Blade is ready. He knows where his enemy is and he's
set on revenge. But it's going to be tough. Hawk has
retreated to his hideout and surrounded himself with
protection. How is Blade going to get past the guards
and confront the man who has destroyed his life?

Because nothing else will do now. The days of running
are over. It's got to be face to face, just the two
of them, and losing is not an option. The question
is—does Blade have the will and the strength to
defeat the man who has always won?

The eighth and final title in this ground-breaking
series from Tim Bowler, the Carnegie Medal-
winning author of *River Boy*, *Starseeker*, *Frozen Fire*
and *Bloodchild*. Blade can feel victory within his
grasp, but is he risking all for nothing?

tim bowler

Other Books by Tim Bowler

book 8

tim bowler
winner of the carnegie medal

BLADE
RISKING ALL

OXFORD
UNIVERSITY PRESS

OXFORD
UNIVERSITY PRESS

Great Clarendon Street, Oxford OX2 6DP

Oxford University Press is a department of the University of Oxford.
It furthers the University's objective of excellence in research, scholarship,
and education by publishing worldwide in

Oxford   New York

Auckland   Cape Town   Dar es Salaam   Hong Kong   Karachi
Kuala Lumpur   Madrid   Melbourne   Mexico City   Nairobi
New Delhi   Shanghai   Taipei   Toronto

With offices in

Argentina   Austria   Brazil   Chile   Czech Republic   France   Greece
Guatemala   Hungary   Italy   Japan   Poland   Portugal   Singapore
South Korea   Switzerland   Thailand   Turkey   Ukraine   Vietnam

Oxford is a registered trade mark of Oxford University Press
in the UK and in certain other countries

British Library Cataloguing in Publication Data

Data available

ISBN: 978-0-19-275601-5

1 3 5 7 9 10 8 6 4 2

Printed in Great Britain

Paper used in the production of this book is a natural,
recyclable product made from wood grown in sustainable forests.
The manufacturing process conforms to the environmental
regulations of the country of origin.

For Rachel
with my love

Dawn sky, dead sky. Deep, dronky grey. Clouds, no sun. Just the dream of it, somewhere far away. But you know what, Bigeyes? I never seen a dawn so beautiful.

Take my eyes off it, stick 'em on the house.

Cos that's what matters. That's where he is. My enemy. In his castle, his nest. Hawk's nest. He's got loads of 'em, Bigeyes. You bet. All over the country, all over the world. But this one? Out here in this remote spot?

He only ever uses it for one reason. And you can probably guess what that is. If you've been paying attention. You know enough about the bastard to work out his obsession.

Yeah, OK, he's got more than one. Power, that's a big 'un. He loves that, needs it. Money, that's another. Possession, number three. You name it, he wants to own it. Antiques, paintings, boats, cars, planes, whatever. He wants the whole stack.

And people.

Oh, yeah. He's into owning people big time. And he doesn't just want part of you. He wants all of you, good and total. When he's got you like that, he's one happy boy. And one dangerous gobbo. Cos you're drummed. You don't even breathe unless he says so.

And then there's the Game.

Hawk's big obsession.

To smash up this world and build it again, in his own stinking image. Him and his fellow slime. Playing for the highest stakes of all. Yeah, he wants all that. And more. Cos you know what? There's something he aches for, Bigeyes.

And it's constant. And when things are bad, that's

when he craves it most. When he's choking with anger, like he is now, that's when he's got to have it. So he comes here. To make sure he can have what he wants.

In secret.

Once upon a time, I was that secret. The reason why he came here. Not any more, thank Christ. It's some other victim now. But I can't be thinking about that. I got to stay focused.

Right, Bigeyes. Check out the house.

Go on, check it good.

All quiet. Just a few lights on. There'll be more soon. Give 'em time. They just got here, remember. Hawk's copter sitting on the gravel. No cars yet. But they'll be on their way. Hawk comes here for solitude, but it's not proper solitude.

It's solitude as he sees it.

Solitude with bodyguards.

Cop a glint over the house. Bigger than you thought, right? Looked small from a distance, I know. And it's not huge, not by Hawk's standards. Even so, it's got plenty of rooms. And there's two you got to know about.

Can't see either from here.

But you can picture 'em.

First up, look over to the right. Bottom of the house. Check out the porch. Now let your eyes flick over the gravel towards where Hawk's parked his copter. Stop just before that and let your mind dig down. Cos your eyes can't go there.

Under that very spot.

There's a bunker. Hawk had it built special. Told me himself, back in the days when I was in favour. You're thinking it's for protection. Well, maybe it was in the beginning.

But he doesn't need it for that. Not really. Got too much shit looking after him already. So he uses the bunker for something else. Yeah, Bigeyes, same again. Use your imagination.

You'll have to anyway. Cos we're not hitting the bunker. We're hitting the other room you can't see. It's hidden from here by the wing of the house. But we can't go for it now. Too dangerous. The grinks just got here so we can't snap straight in. They got their rituals. And the first ritual's to make sure the boss is safe.

So we got to pull back for a bit and . . .

Shit, sooner than I thought. Two grinks standing in the porch. I thought we'd get a few minutes to wig it but they're out here already. They'll be sniffing round the building, sheds, outhouses. And this fence I'm hiding behind.

Come on. We got to rip.

Check the bag, make sure everything's cute inside. Close it up, slip into the trees, find the darkest spot, bung a glance back. No sign of the grinks. Just glimpses of the house in the gaps between branches. But they'll grub out this little wood, no question.

I can't stay here.

On through the trees, stop at the edge, think. Got to watch my step here, Bigeyes. It's kind of thrown me, Hawk turning up same time I did. I never expected him to do that. Wasn't even sure he'd come at all.

I had two plans. If there was nobody here, I was going to break in and wait. Day, two days, whatever. Case the bastard showed. And if he was already here—like I hoped he would be—then I'd watch for a chance and snick in when I could.

Probably at night.

But now it's different, with him turning up right

this second and his grinks out bumming the turf already. I got to blast out for a bit, let 'em scout round, find nothing, then pick my time and creep back.

Skirt round the trees, keep 'em between me and the house. Stone wall just ahead, snaking up the side of the valley. I had this in my head, Bigeyes, when I was trigging here. I remember it from the past.

And there's a spot up there where I think I can hide. Just hope I've remembered it good. Or guessed it good. Cos I've never hidden there before. Just seen it from the house. Anyway, let's give it a fizz.

Over to the wall, crouch close, check over. House looks older from this angle. Don't ask me why. Maybe it's the dronky grey dawn. Seems to be getting darker rather than brighter.

That might help me a bit. Got to hope so. More lights click on. Most of the downstairs rooms lit up now, couple upstairs. Here goes another. Curtains whipping back, windows opening.

And more grinks cutting into the grounds.

I don't like this, Bigeyes. The two I saw in the porch have come round and now there's two more joining 'em. Big gobbos, hard slugs. Another light goes on upstairs. Nothing on the top floor yet. All dark, curtains still drawn.

Check out the gobbos.

Talking in a group, like they're planning who checks where. I can't wait for this. Some are going to be heading this way and there's no point hanging round. But now we got more trouble.

Motors turning up, three of 'em, flash-looking slammers. Fourth motor further off, purring up the lane. They pull in, nose round Hawk's copter, stop. Clunk of doors and more beef gets out.

I'm counting fifteen.

Jesus, Bigeyes, what's happening? He never used to bring this many. Not out here. That was the whole point. He wasn't supposed to need to. Cos this was his retreat, his little secret den. His nest, like I told you. That was what he liked best. He could get away here, keep things simple, cos only a few of his most trusted grinks knew about this place.

Only now I'm starting to get it.

And it chills my heart.

Cos it's going to make everything that much harder. Might even make it impossible. And I'm angry with myself, Bigeyes, cos I should have seen this coming. It's so bloody obvious now. Why didn't I crack it before?

Hawk's expecting grime. Course he is. I mean, face it, Bigeyes—doesn't take a buzzbrain to work it out. He's got shit flying all around him, right? The gangster bojos are blowing blood, the porkers are making arrests.

The honest porkers anyway, not the bent bastards like Jakes.

But the point is—there's enough grime out there now to make Hawk nervous. He knows they all got stuff on him. And what's worse is he knows the kid they got it from. So, yeah, even out here he's expecting trouble.

He might even be expecting me.

The grinks are still standing there, naffing. Some of the beef joins 'em from the cars. Check the numbers again. Ten standing there now. Rest of the gobbos are piling into the house.

But ten's enough.

They're splitting. Two cutting off left to the sheds and outhouses, two to the barn, three round the front of the house, three off to the fence where I was hiding. And they won't stop there. They'll climb over and work through the trees.

Then check this way.

I got to shift.

And I got to keep low. Not just from the grinks outside but from the house. If I could spot the hiding place from the window, someone else can too. And cop a glint of me clambering up the valley.

Up, up, fast as I can, low as I can.

Check over my shoulder.

House is still hidden by the wall, so I reckon I'm cute from that angle, for the moment anyway. What's really bombing my head is the grinks crabbing over the fence. I can't straighten up and look for 'em. Too risky. But they'll be into the trees by now.

If I don't make it over the rise quick, they'll be out in the field and they'll have a bung-clear view up the slope. With me on it.

Christ.

Scramble on, breathing hard. Getting tired now,

really tired, and the pain from where those other grinks hurt me yesterday's cranking up. Aching all over and head's thumping like it wants to break open. I grip the bag, push myself on.

Check behind again.

I can see the trees clear, and the field to the right, even the little track I cut across when I triggered here during the night. Still no figures breaking out. Jesus, Bigeyes. I just need 'em to stay in the trees a bit longer.

Few seconds, that's all.

Stay in the bloody trees.

I stumble on, up, up. Here's the top of the rise. Stumpy ground, rocky outcrops, grassy hillocks. Stone wall twists up and over the hill. Second wall branches off it to the right.

Check back.

And now there's figures below. All three gobbos. Light's picked up and I can see better. Trouble is, so can they. I drop to the ground, take a moment, lift my head, just enough to fix 'em with my eyes.

Mean-looking dregs. They'll all have guns. Not showing 'em, not here, case some farmer or local dronk comes blundering by. But they'll be armed. Trust me. Don't think any of 'em's clapped me.

Shit, they're coming up the hill.

Crawl over the edge of the rise, bundle the bag into my chest, roll down the other slope. Boulder just below to break my fall. I brace myself for the thump. Mustn't make a sound. But I can't help it. Thing slaps me so hard I give a yelp.

I lean back against the rock, catch a breath, listen. They won't have heard. It wasn't that big a yelp. Take another breath, scramble down the hill. Yeah, Bigeyes, I know what you're thinking. I'm thinking it too.

So much for the hiding place.

Well, it looked like one from the house. That's all I can say. Yeah, I know. It was a long time ago. But I remember what I saw. And it looked like there was a little gully thing just below the stone wall. Kind of a nook where I thought I could keep out of sight. Wasn't expecting this other slope to be so flat and wide open.

So there's only one thing left.

Never mind what it is. No time to explain. Down the slope, fast, fast. Got to push hard now, really hard.

Moment they hit the top of the rise, they'll clap me. Unless I can get to what I've just seen.

The only place left to hide.

Trouble is, ground's rocky. One slip and I'll snag an ankle, and that's game over. Push on anyway, hard as I can. Got to risk it. No point hanging back. Turn an ankle and I get caught. Move slow and I get caught.

So what's the point hanging back?

Got to blast down this slope.

Halfway to the bottom. Check back to the rise. No figures yet. Maybe they won't come this far. Maybe they'll just climb up part of the other side, enough to get a view round the house. Maybe that's all Hawk wants.

Yeah, right.

I'm zipping myself over with that one.

They'll hit the rise. No question. They'll do this proper. And I got to be out of sight. But here's the broken bit of the wall I spotted from the top. Scramble over it, panting hard. And here's the other thing I saw.

Gorse.

Big spiky patch. Wish it was thicker but I'll have to

chance it and crawl in. It might just block the sight of me. Trouble is—I don't know. I might be easy to see. And even if I'm not, there's no other place to hide on this slope, so if the grinks are grubbing out thorough, this is the first place they'll slam.

But there's nothing I can do now. Nowhere else to go.

Onto my knees, hugging the bag with one arm, prodding a way through the spines with the other. Jesus, Digeyes. I hate this stuff. Damp and prickly. Smells too, yuk. Check over my shoulder, peer through the spines.

Glimpses of sky, hill, the broken wall.

Too many glimpses.

This won't work, Bigeyes. If I can see out, the grinks can see in. Got to go deeper, find a place where there's no glimpses out. Trouble is, I don't know if you get that with gorse. Specially this time of year. It looked thick from up top but down here, in the middle of it, I'm crawling about and crawling about and I still feel like any neb with half an eye can see me.

Here's a better clump.

Thicker, darker. More prickly, more smelly, but who

cares? It's all that's left. And now I got no choice. Got to stay right where I am and not move. Cos there's voices coming close.

Gobbos.

Got to be those three grinks. Can't see 'em. I'm curled up, tight as I can, bag locked against my chest, back to the wall. And the voices are coming from there. Don't ask me if they can see me through the gorse, cos I don't know. And I don't dare move my head to look. Got to just trust now.

And hope.

Voices getting louder, footsteps tramping nearer. Then everything stops. And suddenly there's nothing. Just me curled up, in the gorse, in the silence.

Waiting.

Like them.

Just a few feet away.

I can feel 'em. They haven't climbed over the wall, but they're close. Don't ask me how I know. Leaning on the rubbly brick, I'm guessing, looking over, checking the gorse. Checking me, maybe. Grinning to each other at the sight of the kid curled up in the gorse, thinking no one can see him.

Sound of a chuckle, another. Burst of sniggering, then a scramble of feet, grunts. They're making their way over the broken wall. No mistaking that. Tramping again, swish of gorse, somewhere behind me.

Then a voice.

'Top field. Just down from the wall. The gorse.'

I'm shivering now. Can't stop it. I stay curled up, tight as I can. Nothing else to do. No point moving. But I want to look round. I want to fix 'em, if only to glare back. Voice comes again.

'Yeah, OK.'

He's talking on a phone.

I take a breath, force myself to stay still. More tramping, circling the gorse now. Flick my eyes about, peer into the spines. Nothing clear to see, just shadowy forms edging round. The voices have stopped. Then I catch a new sound. And I recognize it straight up.

The copter. It's taking off. I curl up tighter, listen. Sound's getting louder, closer. I look up and catch a new shadowy form, hovering over me like a great bird. Laughter again, hooting even.

I clench my fists. Yeah, you bastards. You're loving

this, aren't you? The easiest job you ever had. Stroll up the hill, down the other side, and there's the kid, shivering in the gorse.

Waiting for you.

Hawk's going to love you boys so much.

The bird-shadow looms closer. Hasn't landed yet. Still hovering, but it's getting lower all the time. I stare up. Still hard to make the thing out with all these spiny little branches in the way. But I don't need to.

I can picture everything.

And right now I'm picturing a face. Hawk's face. He'll be at the controls. Oh yeah, you bet. The grinks probably spotted me here from the top of the rise, rang the house, sauntered down.

And the big man's come in person. Like he would.

He's in that copter right now. I know it.

And I'm dead.

Copter moves closer. It's not just the engine getting louder, the shadow getting bigger. It's the spines of the gorse. They're dancing in the rushing draught. More laughter from the gobbos, more hooting.

I curl up tighter. Don't know why I'm bothering. Might as well lie on my back, wait for 'em to pluck me out. Cos they can't miss me, not now. The gorse is swaying, bouncing, over me, round me, gaps opening on all sides. I'm like water pouring out of a sieve.

I think of the bag, what's in it. If I'd been quicker, got myself ready, I could have used that. Now it's a wasted gig. The gobbos down here'll see what I'm doing and stiff me before I can prime up. Before the copter gets down, before Hawk even gets out.

But nobody grabs me.

Nobody even touches me.

And there's a change in the sound above me.

The copter's not coming down. I can tell from the buzz of the engine. It's climbing again. I whip a glance up. It's turned back into a shadow, cos the gorse has closed round me again. The other shadows are moving too, some disappearing, some cutting round after the others.

And suddenly there's no shadows at all.

No voices, no laughter. Just the drone of the copter, fading.

And the gorse lying still.

I'm trembling bad, squeezing the bag tight like before. I don't get it, Bigeyes. They must have seen me. They can't be blind. I take a breath. Too scared to move. I don't feel safe here but it's all I got. I want to just stay curled up, in this spiny darkness. But I can't.

I got to know what's happened.

Push back the branches, peer through.

I counted wrong. There's twelve of 'em. But maybe some came up from the house separate, climbed over that other wall. Yeah, there's a stile. They probably trigged over that way.

Whatever.

Twelve of the bastards.

And they're heading off right, backs to me.

Copter's wigged it over the house, hovering over the fields on the other side. Check back to the gobbos. Still walking on, but spreading out now, covering the ground all the way up to the top wall and down to the base of the valley.

I can only guess what happened.

They missed me, Bigeyes. They just bloody missed me. Came this way to grub out the place. Normal routine. Hawk always makes his dronks do that. Gathered round the gorse, had a few laughs. Copter comes over, checking too.

Grinks in the copter fly down, hover over the gorse. Bit of larking with the dronks on the ground. Nobody's checking the gorse. Cos they're all looking at each other. Copter flies off. Gobbos on the ground trig on.

Just guessing.

Whatever happened, I was lucky. And I got another slam at this thing. Problem is, I can't stay here. Got away with it once but it's too risky. They should have smacked the gorse. They will next time. Probably poke it about.

I got to pull back, find another place to hide, wait there till dark. Yeah, Bigeyes. We got to be patient. There's that many grinks swilling round, I'll never get past 'em in daylight.

Hawk's nervous. That's clear. Never seen so many minders round this place. And he won't have been in the copter. I was wrong about that. He'll be holed up in the house, making sure he's safe. Then waiting for his treat to be brought to the bunker.

I got to play this cute.

Check out through the spines. Copter's way off to the right, grinks still ploughing on, backs to me. Clutch the bag, crawl back through the gorse, check out the broken wall. Nobody standing there, nobody near. Nobody I can see anyway.

I got to go for it, Bigeyes.

Out of the gorse, keeping low, scramble over the break in the wall, crouch against the other side, check round. Nobody up on the rise, nobody in this part of the valley. Bung a glance up the far hill. Looks like a fence running along the top.

Don't ask me what's behind it.

Just got to hope there's somewhere I can go to ground, stay out of sight, crack out the hours till dark. Down the hill, low, close to the wall. Ground's rocky like before but it's getting mushier with every step.

Bottom of the valley. Little stream trickling along it. Never saw that from the top. Kick through it, up the other side towards the fence. Check behind. Still nobody watching from the opposite hill.

But I'm choking about that copter. Can't see it but it sounds closer than it was. Think it's heading back towards those other grinks. Jesus, Bigeyes. I got no chance if it rips over here.

Engine's getting louder. I push against the wall, twist my head. Still no sign of it. Creep on, up the hill towards the top. Copter's hovering, somewhere over the field beyond the wall. I keep moving, up, up, up.

Top of the hill's getting closer. Fence is clear to see now and it's a whack to climb, thank Christ. Just hope I can get to it without being clapped. On, on, tight to the wall.

Sound of the engine changes again. Now's the moment. Copter's spinning back towards the house. Push on up the slope, stop at the fence. This is where it gets scary, Bigeyes. Cos they can see me best up here.

Ease my head up, check over the wall.

The grinks I saw earlier are trigging back towards the gorse. Watch close, Bigeyes. See? I was right. They smack the gorse, poke through it. Move on towards the break in the wall.

This is it. Got to move now. Before they hit this part of the valley. Slime up the fence, low as I can, ease over the top, down the other side, duck below the level of the rise.

Check what's in front of me.

And oh, you beauty. Another valley—and trees. Nice big patch too. Come on, Bigeyes. Down the slope, steady, steady. Got to watch my footing. Still rocky ground. But it's flattening out quicker than the other slope, and here's the first of the trees already. Dive into the dark, pick a path through the gloom.

Yeah, just what I want. Trees tight together. We'll find a spot on the far side. Stuff as much turf as we can between us and the grinks. Don't suppose they'll come grubbing out here. They'll check for grime close to the house, make sure everything's cute for Lord H, then pull back.

And watch.

All the time.

Yeah, Bigeyes. It's going to be a bum gripe getting into Hawk's nest. But I'm going for it. I'm telling you. I haven't come all this way just to blast off again cos it's a spitty gig. I got one reason for being here. And no reason for being anywhere else.

Here's a good spot.

Big, tall trees, close-packed, high canopies. Not much in the way of leaves, but I can't help that. Wrong bloody season to be doing this. Check round. Got to choose the best one.

This'll do. Bastard to climb cos there's no low branch and the trunk's got nothing to snag onto. Yeah, Bigeyes, you got it.

I want a bastard to climb. So no one'll expect to see me up there.

And this one's a proper dingo.

Come on.

Open the bag, check through. Still can't believe it, Bigeyes—Ezi giving me everything I asked for. Didn't think I'd get the plum shit, never mind the other stuff. But it's all in the bag. Bless his wicked heart.

Pull out the rope, check it over. Light, strong, just like I wanted. Tie a few stop-knots at one end, give it some weight. Peer up, fix the bottom branch, aim, chuck. Rope curls over first go, loops down the other side. Flick the rope a few times, ease the weighted end further down, reach up, grab it.

Hook the rope through the bag handles, tie the ends together, check everything's firm. Squeeze the rope-lines into one, take a breath, haul myself up, slow, steady. No need to rush. And just as well.

I'm panting already.

Jesus, Bigeyes, this is tough. I used to be great at climbing. I probably still am. You don't lose that. But I'm feeling the strain bad. Head's still pounding. So's my body. It's almost like I forgot the pain when I was trying to get away from those dungpots back there.

Now there's no grinks, the pain's blamming me again.

Push on, up the rope. Got to reach that first branch. It's easy after that. And I can stay hidden up there, hopefully. Just got to reach that first branch. On, on, closer, closer. Here's it is, just a bit further.

Reach up, clap hold of the branch.

Bark feels cold, unwelcoming. But I don't care. Drag myself up the last few inches, flop over onto the branch, lie there, gasping. Then I hear it again.

The sound of the copter.

Buzzing close. Check up through the canopy. Bits of the sky visible but not much. I chose good with this tree. But I better stay down here for the moment, let the copter skip past. Peer down.

Bag's swinging at the bottom of the rope. Haul it up, slip it free, coil the rope, stuff it back in the bag. Check up again. Copter's over the trees now but it's off to the left. No way they can see me down here. Long as they don't come any nearer.

But it's OK. They're flying off already towards the house.

And I'm moving too, up, up. I've seen what I want, right near the top. Check it out, Bigeyes. See the bit I mean? OK, we'll get a bit closer. Up, up, nice and slow. Right, here we are. See it now?

Proper little snug. Well, all right. Not a snug. A snug's somewhere comfy. Warm and safe with food and a good bed. And books. Jesus, yeah. Books. I bloody miss books. So I guess this isn't a snug. But I'll tell you what, Bigeyes.

It's the nearest thing we got out here.

And it's not bad. Little cradle of branches to hold me firm. I could fall asleep up here and not slip out. But I won't be falling asleep. No chance of that. I'm too cold, too cranked up. Too frightened.

That's right, Bigeyes. No point zipping you over.
I'm choked out. Ease myself into the cradle, lean back,
pull the bag onto my chest.

Close my eyes.

Yeah, my friend. I'm scared like I've never been
scared before. Freaked out of my brain. I suppose I
shouldn't be. Cos think about it. I mean, I've done
what I'm doing so many times.

And I was younger back then. Dead young. But I
still went out and did the business. Hawk would give
me some target. Just a name, bit about where to find
the bastard, anything I needed to know to slam the
gig.

Then leave the rest to me.

So how many times have I waited like this? Eh?
Lost count. Honest, Bigeyes, I've lost count. Yeah, I
know. You're thinking about the list I wrote for Bannerman, all the dronks I killed. You're thinking there's
the number. Count that.

But I can't. Cos there's more.

There's the targets I never hit. I went for 'em,
planned the gig, set it up, waited like this, and never
got lucky. For whatever reason. I was good, Bigeyes,

but I didn't plug every dronk I went for. And when I failed, I paid for it with Hawk.

Oh yeah, you bet.

But here's the point. I've been here before. Lots of times. Waiting, thinking, feeling scared. So why's this different? Yeah, dimpy question. Don't know why I'm even asking. Cos it's easy as piss to tell you.

It's different cos of the target. Cos it's Hawk. And it's different cos of the other thing. The thing that chewed Ezi up when I told him what I need. The thing I got in this bag. It's different cos of that.

I'm scared, Bigeyes.

Almost too scared to move.

But I'll tell you one thing. I'm clear about what's right. What I got to do, what I must do, what I bloody will do. Long as I can find the spit. If anything's going to make me move, it'll be that.

Knowing what's right.

Take a breath, a long breath. Keep my eyes closed. Feel the pain go on, in my body, in my heart. Yeah, that's it, Bigeyes. Knowing what's right. But here's something. When did I start knowing what that was?

When I met Becky? Cos you bet she told me. Oh, yeah. She was just like Ruby for talking straight. Only it didn't work, did it? Cos I kept on doing what was wrong. So maybe it didn't come from Becky. I heard what she said but I took no notice.

So when did I know, eh? I mean, when did I know proper?

When I met Mary? Or Jaz?

Can't answer that, Bigeyes. But you know what I'm starting to think? I reckon I knew the answer long before. From the moment I was born almost. I knew it was wrong I got no memory of my parents. That they dumped me outside that stinky home. I knew it was wrong what happened to me inside.

And afterwards.

Specially with Hawk.

I knew that was wrong. All of it. Didn't need some-one to come and tell me. And that's my point, Bigeyes. You know right and you know wrong. You're born knowing it. Question is—how do you deal with what you know?

Can't answer that either.

All I know is—I didn't deal with it good. Didn't

deal with anything good. If I had done, I wouldn't be here, shivering in a tree. Hungry, cold, hurting, scared.

Getting ready to kill.

Again.

Another breath. Another shiver.

I'm freezing up, Bigeyes. And I don't just mean in my head. Pull the coat tight round me. Should have done this better. Should have got more food inside me before I plugged the car in the lake. There was a place back there I could have called at, just before I hit the country lanes. Maybe got some soup.

But I wasn't thinking.

I just wanted to get here, see if Hawk had showed.

But there's no point glumming. Got to bottle up and get through today. Open my eyes, look round. Tips of the branches moving. Sound of a bird singing off to the right. Don't know what type. Peer round into the trees beyond. Singing goes on but I can't see where it's coming from.

Gone quiet now.

No sounds anywhere. Just the fear murmuring inside me. Touch of rain on my face. Look up, let it patter over me. Feels cold but it's only light. Shouldn't be a problem, long as it doesn't last. Tuck the bag inside my coat to keep it dry.

Close my eyes again. Got to rest now, Bigeyes. Got to get calm, get cool, focus. Cos I'm not going to sleep. No chance of that. But I'm wrong. I fall asleep like I'm wrapped up in a blanket. And I stay asleep, a long, long time.

When I wake, the rain's stopped and there's mist all around.

And voices at the base of the tree.

Gobbos. No prizes for guessing what kind. Twist my head, check down. Three figures standing there. Yeah, grinks, no question. Not looking up. Don't think they've clapped me. Not acting like they have. I'm guessing they're just grubbing round like before.

But this is close.

Got to just hope I chose the right tree. Like I told you, it's a bastard to climb, so they might just slop past without checking up. But if they're doing their job cute, they'll cop a glint this way.

Still standing there, peering round, ground level. I hold my breath, watch. Good thing I'm high up but I'm still visible, even with the mist down.

Move on, you clapheads.

They don't. Just stand there, bottom of the tree, one of 'em munching an apple. I recognize him now. He stamped through the gorse earlier. More voices— shit. Coming from the left. Gobbo with the apple calls out.

'Over here!'

Mutter from the other voices, and now I see 'em. Two more gobbos. Heavy dronks. Jesus, Bigeyes. This is bad. Got to keep still as I can. Only now there's a bird chirping up. Bloody robin, sitting on the next branch. I glare at him.

Cut it out, birdy.

He doesn't.

I peer down at the grinks. All five together now, same spot. Someone's got to look up any moment. I make my body small as I can. Grinks go on naffing, robin goes on chirping. Then a shout below.

'There! Up in the tree!'

I stiffen.

Guffaws below, a big throaty sound. I don't dare look. Just start shivering. Sound of a shot, another. Nothing hits me. Robin flies off. And then there's silence.

But only for a second. Guffaws again, hard, brutal. I make myself peer down. And there they are, all the grinks together, playing football.

With a dead squirrel.

I twist my head back, make myself even smaller. The laughter goes on, then fades away. I wait, go on waiting. No more sounds below. I take a breath. Got to look again, Bigeyes. Got to force myself.

I hesitate, check down.

No sign of the grinks.

Just the squirrel, lying still.

The robin flutters back. Doesn't bother singing. Just perches there, fixes me, stays quiet. I lean back in the cradle, peer round. The branches are dewy and the colour's fading from 'em.

Air feels still.

Like it's scared too.

I clench my fists. I feel so weak, so helpless. But there is one thing on my side—the mist. And night's coming on. Yeah, Bigeyes. I slept through most of the day. Don't ask me how that happened. But I did it. So I guess this is it.

No holding back.

It's time to hit the gig.

Check down, listen. No sign of the grinks, no sound either. I give it five minutes, ten, fifteen—but now I'm bottling. One last check—all quiet below. Darker too, mistier.

Look round for the robin.

Gone. Never saw him wig it. Too bad. I wanted to say goodbye.

Stretch my arms, legs, pull the bag out from under the coat. Climb back down to the lowest branch, feed the rope ends round it, through the handles of the bag, tie 'em together, let everything fall. Wait a moment, grab the rope, squeeze, shin down to the ground.

Squirrel's by my right foot. I bend down, look it over. Half its head blown off by the bullet. I feel the tears come. Don't know why. I should be able to crack this. But then I get it.

The fluffy little toy.

Squirrel Nutkin.

Jaz had a Squirrel Nutkin. Last time I saw her. Last time I'll ever see her.

I straighten up quick, flick my eyes off the corpse. Got to move, got to act. It's not a time for crying. Not now, not ever again. Untie the rope ends, hook the bag free, drop it on the ground.

Stare at it.

Take a breath.

Feel the stillness in the air. Rope's still loose over the branch, both ends hanging down. Not moving, not swaying, not even a bit. I reach out, snap one end tight in my hand, pull. Whole thing comes wriggling down, falls in a heap over the bag and the dead squirrel.

Feel the stillness again. And the fear.

Bend down, coil up the rope, rest it back on the ground. Pick up the bag, open it, look inside. It's all in here, Bigeyes. Everything I need now. My past, my present, my future.

All in this bag.

Tip it up, empty everything out, stare down.

I'm breathing too fast. I should be calm, in control, like I used to be. Even when I was scared, I made sure

I was in control. I take a moment, make myself breathe slow, force it, in, out. Count, you claphead. Count the seconds, count the breaths.

Slowing down a bit.

Not enough but a bit.

I go on counting breaths, in, out, in, out. Stare round at the trees. Dark and misty, yeah, yeah. Just how I want you. Just how I want everything. A last slow breath, heave it in, heave it out.

Now forget about breathing.

Get your stump moving.

Bend down, check everything over. Going to take a few minutes, Bigeyes. Got to make sure everything's as it should be. But Ezi was right. It's no big deal handling this kit. Anyone could do it. Even you.

But I take my time.

Oh, yeah. I'm doing this right, Bigeyes. I'm taking all the time I need to get ready. Five minutes, ten minutes. Last check over. One more for luck. OK, I'm cute to go.

Bag's empty now. Got everything I need on me. Just the rope to sort out. Tie it round my waist, stuff the bag under some leaves. Straighten up, see the squirrel lying there. Bend down again, look over the body.

It's so dark and still. Hard to think it ever had life inside it. I feel the ghosts come back. The pictures I can't bear to see. I reach down, touch the fur. Think of Jaz again.

Stand up, trembling.

'Move,' I mutter.

Last check over the kit. All in place.

'Move,' I say again.

And I'm off, into the darkness, into the mist.

And suddenly it's like I'm awake. Like I've been asleep, deep deep under, and I've just woken up, and I'm sharp and quick and ready. Like all my senses have spiked up. Now the gig's started proper.

The old excitement.

The fear, the energy.

I'm still scared. But I'm better now I'm moving, now I'm hunting. And I got big prey. Something I want bad. Through the trees, mist all around now, and getting thicker and mingled with the dark.

I like this.

Yeah, I like it very much.

Voices off to the right. Funny how they don't scare me like they did just now. I shouldn't feel safe down here on the ground, but I do. Somehow I know I can keep out of their way.

Walk on, soft, easy. It's all coming back, Bigeyes. Just like the old days. I was choking up in the tree. No question. Choking my head to bits. But I'm cool as a knife edge now. Cool as a blade. Cool as Blade even.

Yeah, cool as Blade.

Voices getting nearer. I stop, crouch, listen. Still don't feel scared. It's like fear's just blasted out. I'm crouching and listening, and the grinks are getting nearer, and I'm still not scared. Cos I just know they won't see me.

Here they come.

Four gobbos. Can't see 'em, but I can sense 'em. And the number of 'em. It's not just the voices. It's the whole feel of 'em. Yeah, Bigeyes, I got my instinct coming back. And about time too.

Cos I need it.

Shadows in the trees, off to the right. Yeah, I know.

Looks like one big blobby bastard. Well, it's four grinks. Don't ask me how I know. I just do. Come on. We're splitting right.

Round the side of the oak, crouching. Shadows pass, disappear. I move on. Can't believe how spiked up I am. Feel like I can do anything. And I need this confidence. Cos there's big grime waiting for us.

Left, round the back of where those gobbos came from. Going to have to watch cute. Watch behind, I mean. Cos those dungpots are going to be coming back at some point. So I got to keep a glint over my stump.

But we're all right for now.

On through the trees, and now we're coming to the edge. Stop by the open ground, check round. All I can see is mist and darkness. But I know where the hill is, and the fence at the top.

Up that way, see?

Never mind how I worked it out. Come on.

Into the murk, slow, slow. Can't even see the ground, so I got to watch my step. Ground's starting to rise. What did I tell you? We're climbing and the fence'll be at the top.

Taking an age getting up. Thought we'd be there by now. But no sign of the fence. And now there's voices again. And it's not the gobbos who passed behind us. It's more, and they're somewhere in front.

I'm guessing the other side of the fence.

Stop, listen.

Got to wait. Can't make out where they're coming from. They might not even be moving. Which case I got to be careful. I could walk straight into 'em if I get this wrong.

But there we go again. My old instincts. I got the grinks now, like I'm seeing 'em clear, spite of the mist. They're almost straight in front, just a bit to the right, and they're not moving. Just blobbed there, naffing.

Got a feeling they came out with the gobbos we just saw. Probably Hawk sent 'em out for another grub round. I cut left, up the slope, and here's the fence. Stop again, listen.

Voices off to the right now. Can't see anyone. Just a cloud of mist and dark, and the fence close by, damp under my hand. I go on listening. They're moving. Yeah, definitely moving. Towards the fence.

But not where I am.

I climb over, quick, quiet, drop down the other side. Stop again, listen. Just one voice now. Carries easy. Piece of piss to work out what's going on. He's talking on a mobile to one of the gobbos we saw earlier.

I push on, down the slope to the bottom of the valley, stop. Voices gone quiet. Can't tell if they've climbed over the fence or they're coming back this way. Got to watch myself, Bigeyes. Pretty sure they're not following but I better not hang about.

Left, over to the wall, follow it up the other side of the slope. Here's the broken bit. Climb through it, past the gorse, on, on. That's right, Bigeyes. We're keeping away from the trees we hid in when we first got here. I'm hitting the house from the other side.

More voices—stop, listen again. Different ones. Near too. I crouch down. Still mist and dark all around but I know where I am. I'm in the next field and halfway up the last slope. Top of that there's a wall and then it's down to the house in the dip below.

But that's where these new voices are coming from.

I'm listening cute as I can.

Can't work out how many nebs there are. Just know there's lots. And they're closing in. Left, down to the bottom of the valley, cut along straight, back up the slope towards the wall. Ground's bad here, worse than the other slopes. Got to pick my way over rocks I can't see.

And the mist's getting worse.

Voices moving to the right, down to the spot where I last was. I'm sensing at least five grinks. That means there's lots outside now. The four we first heard, then the ones up by the fence, and now these five. And Christ knows how many others Hawk's sent out.

Jesus, Bigeyes.

He's scared.

He's really scared.

I keep moving, up the last slope. More rocks, more bloody rocks, but I'm getting close. Feeling the weight now, the burden of what I'm carrying. Didn't feel it till now. Don't know why. I kind of forgot it with all these grinks to watch out for.

But the slope's taking it out of me, I'm breathing hard.

And I'm feeling the bloody weight.

Stop, take a moment, get my strength back a bit. Got to stay quiet, stay slick. Cos this is where it cranks up. Here's the wall. And after that there's nothing between us and the house.

Except a few hundred grinks.

Yeah, yeah. Not that many. But enough, OK? Even with all these other bastards outside. There'll be plenty more close to the building. And inside. Hawk's brought a bloody regiment with him. I'm guessing more's turned up while I was sleeping up in the tree.

Stop at the wall, listen again.

No voices. But I'm sensing grinks again. Somewhere near. Can't tell if they're right or left or middle. Just know there's nebs close by. Got 'em. Shadows to the left.

See 'em?

Crouch behind the wall, edge over to a gap in the stonework, peer through. Two grinks. No, three. Carrying guns. Beam of a torch flashes round towards me. I duck, let it pass over. Hear the tramp of their feet in the spongy grass.

Heading the other way.

Straighten up, check round. Run my hands over the wall. Got to watch this bit. Looks crumbly and if a stone crunches out when I'm climbing, some grink might hear it. I test a few stones.

Too risky. Too loose.

More to the right, check again.

This bit's cute.

Up the side, steady, slow. Yeah, you beauty. Nice, firm rock. Just make sure you stay like that. I reach the top, check round, jump down the other side, land soft.

Check again.

Mist swirling, darkness swirling.

But now something else down below.

The lights of the house.

I feel my senses spice up even more. I clench my fists, flex my muscles. I never felt so sharp, so ready. I start to move, slow, down towards the house.

No sign of the building itself. Not yet. Just the lights, and now they're gone. Mist's closed round again. But I got a glimpse, enough to see what's where. And I don't mean the house. I knew where that was anyway.

I'm talking about the part I got to hit.

Cos there's only one way I'm getting in.

I worked it out way back. No question how to snap this. Go straight to him. And I'm not talking about the bunker, Bigeyes. That's where he'll be lots of the time. Maybe he's there now, having his sick fun with some poor shit.

But I'm not talking about that.

I'm talking about where he goes later. By himself. The place where he's always alone. He has to have that place. I know cos he told me, one day when his tongue was loose. He told me he had to have that place. Everywhere he owns, he's got to have one special place.

Where it's just him.

And no one else allowed.

Except me. Yeah, Bigeyes, that's the stinger. He let me in there. Just a few times. When I was in favour. If you can call it that. I don't want to talk about it. But it wasn't often anyway. Like I say, it's his private place. And I'll tell you something, Bigeyes.

He'll need that place right now. Oh yeah, real bad.

I know that cos I know him good. That's why he's come out here. To this remote spot. Cos it's got the two things he wants most. The bunker where he can give out pain—in secret. And the other place.

Where he can rest and plan.

And stay safe.

Alone.

Trust me, Bigeyes. He needs 'em both right now. He's under pressure like he's never been before. Specially now the porkers and the gangster bojos are hitting big. So when he's done with the bunker and sent off the poor bastard he's been whamming in there, he'll head for the other place.

And he'll need that more than ever.

Specially with all these grinks spilling round him. I mean, he wants 'em, yeah, for safety. But don't kid yourself. They're just robots to him. He just uses 'em cos he needs 'em. But deep down, you know what? He hates 'em. Every single one of 'em. They're the same thing to him as they are to you and me.

Scum.

So he'll use 'em for smashing the fields, grubbing for danger. Protection, torture, killing, whatever. But they're nothing to him. Like most nebs are nothing to him. Even his family. Yeah, I mean it. Even them.

Cos that's how it really is, Bigeyes. The only person he loves is himself. So for all his power over other people, he's got no one. No bloody one. Yeah, he owns these grinks, like he owns pretty much everybody in his life. But deep down, he's on his own, trusting no one, hating everyone.

Knowing in his heart they hate him too.

Cos they do. Oh yeah.

Don't ask me how I know.

He's better off dead, Bigeyes.

There's the lights again. I'm just where I want to be. Still no sign of the buildings but the lights tell me what I want to know. Main building's to the right. So we're cutting left, between the outhouses and the stable.

And we got to go cute, cos I'm sensing more grinks nearby.

Yeah, I was right. Cop that shadow. Got it? Never mind, too late. Take it from me. Big guy, just got a glimpse of him. Carrying a rifle. Walk on, low, slow. More shadows—stop.

They're dead ahead, not moving.

Lights behind 'em, twinkling a bit. Gone. Can't see the shadows either but I'm sensing they're still there. Move right, just a bit, now straight on. Got to squeeze round these bastards.

Sound of tramping, off to the left.

Moving away.

But now there's more steps coming from the right. Freeze, crouch, wait. Three grinks plod past, beefbums. Two got rifles, third's carrying a torch. They don't see me, walk on. I let 'em go, wait, move on, closer to where the lights were.

Squashy ground comes to an end and now there's mown grass.

First of the stables. No horses in there now. Hawk used to keep 'em and yeah—you guessed it—he's a brilliant rider. As you'd expect. Brilliant at everything. Brilliant rider, brilliant shot, brilliant whatever.

But he stopped keeping horses here cos he doesn't use the place often enough. And right now I'm glad, cos I can do without snorting noises as I slip past. Up to the first door, check in.

No grinks.

On towards the first of the outhouses. More foot-steps, left and right. I freeze again, listen. None of 'em coming this way. Trig on, past the first outhouse, past the second. Shadow of the barn opens up on my left.

And there on my right's the outline of the main building.

I can see it good now, lights on in most of the rooms. I keep low. Don't think anyone can clap me from the windows cos I'm still swirled in mist and darkness, but I got to play stealth.

Keep back, edge round the building. Barn slips from view and now I'm close to the drive and fore-court. I'm not slamming in this way. Wouldn't make it past the porch. But there's something I got to check. Cos I need to know numbers.

Rough-cut, I mean.

Trig on, low, up to the edge of the house, peer round.

Forecourt opens up. Misty and dark like everything else but there's lights on all around and I can see enough. Hawk's copter's sitting there, and more motors than there were. Loads more. I was right, Bigeyes.

He's got an army keeping watch.

Run my eye back to the copter. And the ground nearby.

Think of the bunker underneath.

Pull back, creep round to where the barn opened up. But now we're keeping close to the house. This is the tough part, Bigeyes, the really tough part. Cos I got lots to do and there's that many grinks here some screamer's bound to drum in and spot me.

So I got to choose the right moment.

And move quick.

Here's the place. Check round. What do you see? Yeah, I know—mist and darkness. And the house. Look again. Look better. OK, point one—no windows. So no one can peer out at me. Point two—look up, Bigeyes.

What do you see?

The wall of the house, climbing, all the way to something you never spotted first time round. And you won't see it now cos of the mist and the dark. But it's there. A little tower at the top of the building. All on its own, built special.

A nest, Bigeyes.

A sanctuary for a dangerous man.

BLADE

Let's go get him.

Over to the wall, crouch close, whip a glance round.
No shadows moving nearby, but voices left and right.
Grinks still grubbing round. Can't tell if they're sliming
this way. Don't think so.

Wait, make sure.

Cos if I go at the wrong time, I'm plugged. I won't
even get close to where I got to be. Like I said. I got to
choose the right moment. No mistakes. And then blast
off quick.

The voices go on. Not getting closer. Not moving
away either. Part of me wants to wait, stay low. But
that's a dronky choice too. Cos they could clap me just
as easy here too, even in the murk.

I'm going for it.

Flick a glance up the wall of the building. Yeah, I
know. You're thinking, bastard to climb, nothing to
hold on to. And you'd be right. But bang your head
back, Bigeyes. Remember that dingo tree and the first
branch? Way out of reach but get to it and everything's cute.

Now look up the building again.

Smooth brick all the way but then—yeah, baby. Little bit of the wall jutting out. Got it? Gargoyle thing on the end. Water runs out of it from that drainpipe above. Building's got loads of stony figures like that. If you look close. But we don't need to.

We just got to hit that one ugly beast. Cos he's our first branch, right? Get to him and we're close to stuff I can climb. Another glance round.

Voices have gone quiet. I don't like that. Didn't hear 'em move off so those grinks could be any-where. Take a breath, another, try to calm down, brace up.

OK, let's do it.

Check over the kit, make sure everything's in its place. Uncoil the rope, tighten the stop-knots at the end. Tie a couple more. Going to need more punch than last time, cos this throw's a bum blitz.

Might not even work at all. Gargoyle's higher up than the branch of that tree. And harder to loop over. And even if I do hook it, the thing might snap under my weight. That's something else I'm trying not to think about.

Stand up, glint round into the mist. All's still, far as I can tell. Take a step back from the wall, check up, swing the rope, swing the rope, swing the rope.

Chuck.

Falls short.

Well short.

Voices again, moving close this time. Slink back to the wall, crouch, wait. They move close, then fade again, heading towards the barn. Stand up, out again, check up, swing the rope.

Up it goes. Falls short like before.

Nowhere near. Now I'm getting worried. Not cos of the rope. I got enough, no question. I gave Ezi the length and he did good, gave me what I wanted. No, Bigeyes, I'm worried about me.

Having the strength.

Cos I'm reeling again.

And it's not just throwing this thing. It's what comes after. The climb. And then the gig itself. Don't ask me how I'm going to manage. I was feeling sharp a moment ago. I'm not now.

Check up again, fix the jutty part of the wall. I can see the gargoyly shape at the end, even in the gloom.

Figure of a boy, screaming. Could almost be me. I narrow my eyes, swing the rope.

The rope snakes up, up, up. Slaps the gargoyle, falls back. But this one was close. Gather in the line, get ready, fix the spot, swing. Up it goes, up, up, loops over the gargoyle, dangles over the neck of the figure, stops.

I take a breath, listen for sounds behind me. No voices, nothing. I want to check over my shoulder cos I still don't feel right. But I don't dare take my eyes off the rope case it slips off.

I stare at it.

Flick the rope.

A little wave rolls up it, all the way to the top, nudges the hanging end down a bit. I see the stop-knots swinging in the dark. Another flick, another little wave ripples up the line and down the other side.

Flick again, and again. Got to play this careful. Flick too big and the rope'll fall off. But it's cute so far, and the stop-knots are falling easy.

Down, down, nice and slow.

Come on, you beauty. Just a bit more.

Closer, closer, the rope still plum over the gargoyle, the knotted end almost in reach.

'Hey! What you doing?'

Gobbo's voice behind me.

I let go of the rope, whirl round, fists clenched. But all I see's mist and dark. No figure anywhere. Footsteps off to the right, tramping this way. I reach for the rope. Got to pull it down before they see it.

But there's no time.

Two shadows moving in from the right.

I scuttle in to the wall, crouch low as I can. Two gobbos, big guys, tanking round the side of the house. They can't miss seeing me. Or the rope at least. It's just hanging there. But they're staring the other way, into the mist.

One of 'em calls out. Same voice I just heard.

'What you doing? And where are you?'

'Over here,' comes an answer. 'Checking the barn.'

And the two grinks disappear from view.

I'm out from the wall, smart. That's it, Bigeyes. Can't wait a moment longer. I got lucky with the gorse. And up in the tree. And now this. But it won't happen again.

Back to the rope, grab hold, calm myself, look up.

Flick, flick, tiny waves shivering up to the top, and still the line stays cute on the jutting wall. And the other end drops lower, lower. Another flick and it's mine. I reach out.

Stop, check myself.

I want to snatch it so bad. But I mustn't. I got to watch every movement, Bigeyes. It could flip off the gargoyle easy. I take a moment, spice my head, check round again. All clear. Take the rope, hold it soft.

Tie both ends together, squeeze the two parts into one line, hold it tight in my fist. Look up, give a tug. Feels firm up there. Pull harder, harder. Nothing gives. So far so good.

Trouble is, I can't see what the top's looped over. I'm hoping it's the hollow in the back of the figure's neck. That should keep it snug. But I can't see for sure. Just got to hope it doesn't slip off when I'm climbing. So I mustn't wriggle about too much.

Anyway, let's go.

Up the rope, shinning slow. I'm trying not to move jerky but it's hard. Least the gargoyle's holding me good. Up, up, up. Check down.

The ground's already disappearing in mist.

More voices below. Can't tell where they're coming from. Seem to be in lots of places at once. Check
up again. Halfway there. I'm moving faster than I
meant to but I can't help myself. I'm so choked about
getting seen from the ground.

Trouble is, the speed's making me swing a bit.

Slow down. For Christ's sake, slow down.

I'm still swinging.

Stop, wait, let the rope stop swinging.

Climb on. Up, up, nice and slow, and here's the
little gargoyle. Like I told you, a screaming boy. Like
looking at myself. Reach up, hook a hand over the
stony back. Thicker than it looks from the ground,
thank God.

Haul myself over, sit astride, breathe hard, check
below. Rope's swinging in the mist. Check up. And
there's more mist waiting.

And somewhere in it, Hawk's nest.

Haul up the rope, untie the ends, coil it round me,
crawl along the stone to where it meets the wall.

Drainpipe running up to the next level—the roof of the main building. No problem getting that far.

It's the last bit that's going to slam me.

If I get it wrong.

But first things first. Ease in to the wall. Flattens out a bit, enough for me to plant my feet. Reach out, grab the drainpipe, test it. Nice and solid. Pull myself up to standing, feet on the stone.

And now up again, clinging to the pipe. Feels cold and wet, bit slippery. But it's still firm and that's all I care about. Up, up, taking it steady. I'm getting tired now, Bigeyes. You better believe it. But I'm holding on, somehow.

And moving up.

Voices far below. Seem like they're from another world. I twist my head, check down. Can't see a thing. All's dark down there and bunged up with mist. Another lucky break. On, on, breathing hard.

Voices still talking. I catch 'em, but not the words. Just the tone. And I think I'm cute. If someone had spotted me, they'd be talking different. Just hope I'm right. Here's the top of the roof.

Shit.

It slants down at me before it flattens out. I didn't clap that from below. And I can't see anything on it to hold. I clutch the end of the drainpipe, check round. Gutter running left and right.

Nothing else in front of me.

Just a slanty, slippery roof.

And beyond that, Hawk's tower rising.

Nothing else for it. Got to go for the roof and hope I don't slip. I pull myself up, feeling for the brackets that hold the pipe to the wall. Gutter's too weak to trust. Up, up, panting.

Half over the edge now, hands down by my waist, clinging to the top of the pipe. I don't dare take 'em off but I know I must. Crab round with my right foot, feel for the highest bracket I can hit.

Got one.

Dig the toe in, push up, grub round with my left foot. Next bracket—got it. Ease a bit higher, but now the brackets have run out and there's only the roof and whatever I can smack on it.

Cos now I got to take my hands off the pipe.

Do it.

Just do it.

I let go, feel my balance start to flip, wave my arms to get it back. Shit, Bigeyes. I'm standing on the brackets, holding nothing. Lean forward, plunge onto the roof, scrabble with my hands for something to hold.

It's almost completely smooth. Tiny grooves between the tiles and that's it. But maybe enough to grip. Got to go for it anyway. I keep my left foot on the bracket, push off with the right, plant it on the bottom tile. It slips off, catches the gutter.

'Ah!'

But the gutter holds firm. Scrape my hands over the tiles, push with my right foot, lunge with my left, and suddenly I'm scrambling up, up, up towards the top.

I don't know how it happened. I'm too scared to remember. But somehow I'm there. I'm sprawled on the flat part of the roof, gasping.

I don't move. I can't move. Not yet. In a moment but not yet. I just stay there, breathing. Waiting for the panic to drain away. Then I roll onto my back.

And see Hawk's tower rising.

And now we got the worst part of all.

Cos this crusher's got no drainpipe, no gargoyle to

hook a rope onto. Just brick. And I got to climb it. But there's one good thing, Bigeyes. And I'm glad my memory hasn't let me down. Cos there's something I remembered from the past.

The bricks are chunky bastards, see? The tower wasn't part of the original building. Like I told you, Hawk had it built special. And he obviously liked these bricks.

Well, so do I, Bigeyes. Cos they're climbable.

I think.

Back on my feet, over the roof to the tower, check round. Just a dusky view of what's below. Glimpses of the ground, no more, like little windows have opened up in the mist and dark and I can see through.

But even where I got glimpses I can't see much.

So I don't reckon they can either.

Lights moving here and there, grinks flashing torches round the house, up on the slopes, over where the trees are. Pretty sure they can't see me up here, even on the tower. I reach out, touch the wall.

Feels cold and damp. Run my fingers along the grooves between the bricks. Better than the tiles but still not much to hold on to, and it's going to be worse with what I'm carrying. But there's nothing else for it.

Take off the rope, drop it on the roof. No good to me now. Done its bit. Check pockets, check the kit. Everything in place. Start to climb.

Slow, real slow, one hand up, other hand up, one foot, other foot. Inch by inch, that's how it's got to be. Least the brickwork's even. Means I know what's coming next. But the holds are narrower than I thought and the bricks are getting damper the higher I go.

Stop, take a breath. I feel so vulnerable, Bigeyes, so scared. I make myself climb on. Up, up, one brick, one victory, another brick, another victory, and on, on, closer to the top.

I know the bit I'm aiming for. It's the one part I'm certain about.

The only way in I can think of.

Where I got a chance of not being found out.

Stop again, take another breath, climb on. And here it is, Bigeyes. See? Little tiny window, just under the top of the tower. There's another one on the other side. Takes you into the bathroom. This one takes us into a storeroom.

And there's a bigger window on the very top of the tower.

A massive one.

But we're not going in that way. You'll soon find out why.

Another breath, a long one. This is the next tough part, Bigeyes. I got to force the window without falling off the wall and without being heard from inside. And here's the gripe—I got no idea if Hawk's in there or not.

All I know is what I can see from here. No light inside the storeroom and no glow under the door to the main room. He could be in there. Could be sleeping. But he shouldn't be at this time. It's not late enough.

So I'm hoping he's somewhere else. But I still don't know for certain. That's the gripe, Bigeyes. He might be at his desk with just a lamp on. And that wouldn't show under the storeroom door.

I brace myself, make sure I got both feet firm on the bricks, both hands tight in the grooves. Ease myself up, just a bit more. Check over the window. Not what you'd call big, is it? But it's enough for me.

Reach out, grab hold of the sill. Check the frame, check the catch inside. Cute little thing but nothing Ezi's burglary tools won't slam. I fix my feet again, make sure they're firm, ease my right hand off the sill, reach into my pocket, pull out Ezi's goodies.

Two minutes later I'm in.

Check round, slow. All's dark, all's quiet. Listen cute. No sound of movement beyond the door. Flick a glance at it. Still no light underneath. Nothing I can see anyway. Look round.

Nothing much in the storeroom. Boots, heavy weather gear. Like I told you, he doesn't use this house much, so he doesn't keep a lot here. Creep up to the door. It never had a lock in the old days.

Still hasn't. Good. And it's not clicked shut either. Even better. Put an ear to it.

Nothing.

Just my breath stealing in, stealing out. I wait a moment, quieten down a bit more. Check the kit over. Check it again. And again. Everything's fine. Everything's plum.

If he's in there, if it's got to be now, I'm ready.

Reach out, stroke the door handle, hold it steady. Ease the door open, just a fraction. Darkness in the gap, then a glimpse of the nearest wall. And the familiar shapes all along it.

Hawks.

Peering down with their dead eyes.

He shot 'em all, Bigeyes. Every one. And he's got more on the other walls. Only hawks in this place. There's different stuff in his other homes. Oh, yeah, you bet. Bear skins, tiger skins, elephant tusks, rhino horns, whatever.

Like I told you, he's an expert shot.

And he loves killing.

He'll have guns up here. We won't see 'em but they'll be here. He's never far from a gun. Ease the door a little further.

More of the wall, more hawks peering down, dark like before. Push the door wider. Glint of glass up above, but I'm not looking at that. I'm checking round into the room.

No sign of the bastard. And not a light on anywhere.

Just the shadows of things I remember so well. And yeah, Bigeyes, I do remember 'em well. I was the only other person ever allowed in here. Cos I was his favourite. And he never had any other. He told me that. And I believed him.

I still believe him.

Never mind why. I just do. And that's why he wants me so bad. Wants me dead, I mean. Cos I'm still his favourite. Yeah, Bigeyes, I still am. Don't ask me how I know. So he wants me dead.

Cos I betrayed him.

I stare out over the shadowy room. The long, wide bed, beautifully made, sheets, pillows, duvet just so. Scent of flowers. Everything neat and special. He'll have done all that himself. Oh yeah. Like he'll have cleaned and dusted the room himself. Cos he always does that in his secret nest. Cos it's like I say.

There's nobody else allowed in here.

And there never has been.

Except me.

I let my eyes move on. The books on the shelves, the ornaments, the pictures, the cabinet with the hunting knives. More dead hawks looking down from the walls. The built-in wardrobes, the door into the bath-room. The desk with the anglepoise, the phone, the ugly stone paperweight.

And then the real reason why he had this tower built.

Check right, Bigeyes. And then look up.

The raised floor, the telescope, the big glass dome above. Yeah, Bigeyes. He comes up here to watch the stars. To sleep under 'em, dream under 'em. And I used to suffer under 'em.

Look up at the sky.

No stars tonight. Just mist and dark. But they're up there, Bigeyes. I know they are. I used to gaze up at 'em when I was here. In other places, I used to close my eyes when he whammed me. If I thought he couldn't see.

But not here.

I used to peer up, through the glass, used to spin my eyes over the night sky, searching for 'em, so I could forget what was happening. And sometimes it worked. When I could see 'em. I wish I could tonight.

Look down again, check over the kit.

Got to stop doing that.

It's all ready. I know it is. I just need my enemy now.

Back to the storeroom, slip in, ease the door almost closed, just a tiny gap. Slump down on the floor, back against the wall, clench my fists, let 'em go. This is the bad time. The waiting time.

Stare round.

I got Becky in my head again. But I guess that's a dimpy thing to say. I mean, think about it, Bigeyes. When's she not in my head? And I wouldn't want it any different.

I got Jaz in there too. Little poppet. And Mary. Beautiful old Mary.

'I love you guys.'

My voice sounds strange in the storeroom. Just a whisper but it's like the words spoke by themselves, out of the darkness.

'I love you guys.'

Silence again. I'm thinking of Poppa now. And Bannerman and Fern. And Ruby and her mates. And Bex. Jesus, Bigeyes, what happened to 'em all? I'm hoping like hell none of 'em got shunted when Jakes stuffed me.

But I can't help 'em now.

I can only do this. Just hope it's enough.

Do something better, Ruby said. Don't jump off a bridge. Do something better. For Becky. Yeah, Rubes, I know. But Hawk's hurt me so bad. You got to understand that. There's some things you never come back from, some things you never forgive.

Do something better. I'll try.

'For you, Becky.'

The words whisper out of the darkness again.

'For you, sweetheart.'

Footsteps climbing slow. I stiffen, stand up, check over the kit again. Lean close to the storeroom door, listen. Footsteps grow louder. A pause. Sound of a key turning, door of the main room opening.

Silence again.

A long silence. Like he's waiting, checking, making sure.

Door closes, key turns to lock it, footsteps start again. Crossing the floor, towards the bed, round the bed, stop. I keep back, away from the gap. He can't see me, I can't see him. But I'm sensing what he's doing.

He's standing still. And I can feel him looking round.

A light flicks on. Not the main light. I can tell. It's the anglepoise. Sound of a chair moving. He's sitting down at the desk. Opens a drawer, closes it, pushes back the chair. Footsteps cut off towards the bathroom.

Running water.

Not a bath or shower. He's filling a basin. I go on listening. I could move now. What's to wait for? It's a done deal. He's on his own. He's even locked the door to the room. All I got to do is get myself between him and the way out.

And make sure I plug him before he whips out one of his guns.

Piece of piss.

But I don't move.

Except my hands. They're moving, trembling. Yeah, Bigeyes. Can't stop 'em. Arms trembling too now, and my legs, shaking like I can't stop 'em. I got to get on with this. Got to do it quick or he'll hear me, or sense me, and then he'll come for me.

I can still nail him if he does.

But I won't have surprise on my side.

And I need that.

To do this right.

But I still can't shift. And now he's moving again. Footsteps like before, out of the bathroom, back into the main room. Wardrobe door opening, hangers sliding. He's changing clothes. Could be going out again.

Too early for bed. Another reason why I got to get out there. But I still can't move. I just go on trembling, listening, aching. Then the light goes off. And the footsteps start again.

Coming this way.

I reach into my pocket, feel for what I want. It's all there, still ready. Just me that's not ready. Got to make myself, Bigeyes. I've come this far. I can't fail now. It's simple. It's so simple.

Everything I need's in this pocket. All I got to find now is a tiny act of courage to go with it. That's all. One tiny act of courage. And it's done. Cos now he's coming.

Step, step, step.

Heading straight to me. Maybe he knows I'm here,

maybe he doesn't. Who gives two bells? I feel my hand relax inside the pocket. Feel the rest of me relax too. I'm OK now, Bigeyes. I'm ready. And here he is.

Step, step, step.

Coming into the storeroom.

But I'm wrong. He's stopped by the door. And it hasn't opened. He's just standing there. Maybe he's listening for me. But I'm wrong again. Cos there's another sound. Steps moving right. And now I got it.

He's walking round the inside of the tower.

And I can crack why. He's checking up, through the glass dome. Seen something in the sky, I'm guessing. And now—yeah. He's making his way up onto the raised floor.

This is it, Bigeyes.

There won't be a better time.

Ease open the door, just a bit, peer round. There he is, like I said, up on the raised floor, gazing up at the sky through the telescope. Wearing a dressing gown. Not aware of me at all. Just the sky. And I don't blame him. Cos look, Bigeyes. Mist's cleared.

And there's stars up there.

Beautiful, beautiful stars.

And a soft, sweet moon.

I take my eyes off 'em, fix Hawk again. He goes on watching the sky. Quick glance round the room. All's as it was. Bed tidy, desk tidy. Clothes put away out of sight. Just him and me. And an empty room.

I slip round the door, walk softly over to the bed, stop, my eyes on Hawk. He's still gazing into the telescope, his back to me. Then suddenly he stiffens, straightens, turns.

And smiles down at me.

I stiffen too. Can't help myself. I keep my face still. Just fix him back, hard as I can. He goes on smiling. Looks relaxed, calm, happy to see me. Like we're old mates. Like it's been too long. Like I should have got in touch.

I go on watching. And not just his face. I'm checking his hands. Pretty sure he's got nothing on under that dressing gown, but it's got two pockets, and like I said—he's never far from a gun.

I keep my hand in my own pocket.

Cos that's the key.

The thing that's in there. That's what nails him. I move my hand round it, squeeze gentle. Ready to go.

He can't beat me on this, Bigeyes. I take a step closer.
Don't need to. I could stand back by the door and still
plug him.

But I want to see his face.

And I want him to see mine.

See it good.

But I go on watching his hands.

He's still smiling, like nothing's wrong. Then slowly
he starts to move, down to the right, off the raised
floor, past the storeroom, back towards the desk,
walking casual, soft eyes watching me.

He doesn't come close.

Just saunters past, well out of reach.

Heading for the desk.

I speak.

'Stop.'

He does. Looks me over. The smiles fades.

'Was that an order?' he says.

The smile comes back.

'Because I don't take orders.'

And he walks on towards the desk. I feel my hand
twitch in my pocket. Doesn't matter, all this. He can
mock, play games. He was always going to do that. I'm

still in control. There's no gun on that desk. Probably is in one of the drawers. Or all of 'em.

But he's not close enough yet. And now he's stopped.

By himself.

Still smiling at me. I go on watching his hands. They're hovering over his pockets. The smile fades again and I see the face that's haunted me for three years. The face that's never loved. And now never will.

He moves his hands. Still calm, relaxed, like there's no hurry. Reaches into his pockets, turns 'em out, shows me they're empty, takes a step back, sits on the edge of the desk.

Watching me.

I stare back at him. It's like he hasn't aged at all. He's just grown younger, stronger, more beautiful. I hate him so much. He speaks.

'So am I the target this time?'

I don't answer. Hawk raises an eyebrow.

'You can't win, you know.'

Somewhere far away I hear the drone of an engine. More than one engine. Hawk catches it too, gives a chuckle.

'More reinforcements. You can never have too many. Especially when there are dangerous killers on the loose.' He looks me over. 'Not that you're really dangerous. To be honest, I find you rather pathetic. I mean, you don't really think you can kill me, do you?'

'You're already dead,' I murmur.

Again he raises an eyebrow. The sound of the engines goes on. Still distant, but getting louder. I don't bother about 'em. Whatever they are, they can't save this bastard. And that's all I care about.

'So what's in the pocket?' he goes on. 'A knife, I suppose.'

I keep my hand in there. Tight, ready.

'Not a knife,' I say. 'Given up on knives.'

'A gun, then.'

I shake my head.

'Too risky. I might miss with a gun.'

Hawk's face darkens. For the first time.

And something passes over his eyes. Something

I've never seen before. A shiver of fear. His gaze moves back to my hand, my pocket. I keep watching his face. Cos he could spring any moment.

The sound of the engines grows louder. Christ knows how many motors he's got rolling in. Bloody convoy, I reckon. But all the backup in the world won't save him now. Cos it's just him and me in here. And that's all I ever wanted.

'What's in the pocket, Blade?' he says.

'A detonator switch.'

I pause, watch, speak again.

'I'm wearing a bomb vest.'

I unzip the coat with my free hand, let him see underneath. He doesn't move, just stares. Sound of car doors slamming, footsteps on the gravel. I nod upwards, towards the glass dome.

'Get ready, Hawk. Cos we're going to the stars together. In pieces.'

I brace myself, start to squeeze the switch—then freeze. Cos suddenly there's a new sound. A small, soft sound. It checks me, fills me with terror. Cos it's not from down below.

It's from inside this room.

Gone quiet again. But I heard it. I know I did. Somewhere near the bed. A small, creeping movement. But it can't be. I checked the room. And I can't check again. Can't take my eyes off Hawk.

Not for one second.

I keep my hand on the detonator switch. It's still half-pressed and me and Hawk are halfway into death. But who else is too? And does it matter? Cos if it's some grink in the room, he can come with us. But what if I'm wrong?

What if it's someone else?

I see the change in Hawk's face.

See the confidence come back.

The smile.

Then catch the sound again. A small, stealthy movement, somewhere to the left. I flick my head round. Can't help it. I know I shouldn't. But I got to know. Whip a glance over the end of the room.

Nothing.

Same as before.

Nobody on the bed, nobody in it, nobody this side of it. But I can't see the other side. Can't see if there's someone creeping along the floor. And I don't get the chance. Cos even as I snap back to watch Hawk, something hard smashes into my face.

I stagger, head spinning. Somehow I stay on my feet. Through a blur I see Hawk bent over the desk. He must have flung the paperweight and now he's digging in a drawer.

I fumble with my right hand. It jerked out of my pocket when I got hit, darted up to cover my face. Couldn't stop it. I try to squeeze it back into the pocket with the detonator.

Crack!

A bullet rips up my wrist. I give a yelp of pain.

Crack!

Another bullet, upper arm.

More pain and now blood's starting to gush. I'm swinging my arm, trying to shove my hand back in the pocket, but it won't go. And here's Hawk striding forward.

Crack!

Third bullet. Ploughs into my thigh.

I go down, hard on my back. The floor thumps the breath out of me. I'm bleeding bad now, fighting blacko, but I keep trying to ram my hand into the pocket. Hawk dives on top of me, pins my right arm back, thrusts the shooter under my coat, feels round the bomb vest till he finds a spot on my body.

Digs the gun-point into me, leans close, hisses.

'Stupid. So stupid.'

His eyes cut into mine.

'Did you really think you could kill me?'

His breath's hot. Yeah, Bigeyes. Hot. It always was. I remember. He shoves the gun point harder against me.

'Really thought you were special, didn't you?'

I don't answer. I can't. I got blood filling my mouth, filling my eyes. He gives a low, animal laugh.

'You were never special,' he growls. 'I'll tell you what you were. You were just another boy off the street. Just another worthless piece of trash. Because that's what you all are. Every single one of you. Worthless trash.'

His mouth curls into a sneer.

'I can't wait to see you die.'

He eases back, just a bit, the gun still hard against me. I know what he's doing. He wants to see better.

Wants to watch me twitch, bleed, flicker, go still. I don't care, Bigeyes. He can watch what he likes now.

There's nothing I can do to stop him.

I just wish I hadn't failed. Cos I should have killed him.

For Becky's sake.

He smiles that smile. The one I know so well.

'Goodbye, Blade,' he whispers.

He skews the tip of the gun towards my heart, then suddenly rears up, the smile twisted off him. I stare up, confused, and see horror in his eyes. He gives a gasp, then falls over me, spluttering.

I stare past his shoulder and see a small boy standing there.

About seven years old, naked. He's got whip-slashes all over his body. And he's holding one of Hawk's hunting knives. It's got blood on it.

Hawk stirs. He's breathing hard, jerky. The boy got him in the lower back but it hasn't killed him. I look up at the kid. He's so like me, Bigeyes. Same face, same eyes, same fear. Yeah, specially that.

I mutter to him.

'Get out of here, boy. Find your clothes and run. Just . . . run.'

Sound of voices outside the room. Gobbos calling out. I'm guessing they heard the shots. Someone bangs the door. I reach down with my left hand, feel for the gun. Got to prise it away before Hawk recovers.

But it's too late.

He's picked up the movement. He gives a moan, whips the gun away from me, thrusts it back under my coat, stabs it against my body. More shouts from outside, more thumping on the door. Getting louder and louder, and now the pain's tearing me apart.

I fix the boy's eyes.

He's all that matters now.

'Run for it,' I mumble. 'Just . . . just . . .'

I hear Hawk snarl, feel him steady the gun.

Then everything goes black.

And stays that way. Doesn't change. Just goes on. An endless black. But I know where I am. Oh, you bet. I recognize this place. I've been here before. It's lonely but it's cool. Just black silence and me.

Or what's left of me. Cos I'm zippo now. A mind moving through nothing. Searching for a way to die. Yeah, that's right. I'm looking for him.

Death.

Scummy bastard.

I met him once, remember? Just after Dig cut my head. Met him close, face to face. He played games with me, spun my brain, put me in his bag, zipped it up—then let me out again.

And I lived.

Bastard.

What's he going to do this time? When he fixes me with his eyes. Cos he's not far away. Don't ask me how I know. I can feel his soft sad breath whispering over me. But I'm cute about that.

I want to die so much.

I can't wait to see him.

But now there's other faces turning up instead. I don't want to see 'em. I want to see Death's face. He's the only gobbo I'm after. But these other ones are crowding round.

'Get lost,' I murmur.

I scowl at 'em, try to brush 'em away. They don't

go. They bustle round. Dark, scary faces. And now I recognize 'em. It's the dronks I killed. Every one. They're moving round me, staring, just staring.

Jesus, Bigeyes.

Is that what Death's got waiting for me? The dregs I plugged with my knife? Is that how you pay back what you owe? You kill these dungpots and then get stuck with 'em for eternity?

They go on moving round me.

Then I catch a voice.

'Blade.'

I wish it was Mary. I remember when she called my name. That time I was blacko and she brought me out. With that sweet Irish voice. But it's not Mary. It's some gobbo.

'Blade.'

I wish he'd shut up. I'm trying to die here.

And I can't with him blabbing.

'Blade,' he goes.

'Piss off.'

He doesn't piss off. Just goes on saying my name.

'Shut your mouth,' I grumble.

I stare at the faces. Still moving round me, but

they're further back than they were. I fix 'em. They're all watching me. And here's something I don't get. They don't look angry. Why not?

They should be steaming at me.

Cos I plugged 'em all.

Yeah, yeah, they were scum. They probably still are scum. Me killing 'em won't have changed that. So why aren't they ripping off at me? Why don't they hate me?

They should. Cos I hate me.

Oh, yeah. I hate me.

'Blade,' says the voice again.

The faces disappear. And it's just blackness again. Only I'm wrong. There's one face left. Can't see it clear. It's kind of hovering over me. And now I'm seeing something else. This face—it's not one of those scumbos.

It's some other face. A face that wasn't there before. Still hard to see in all this black. And now there's another thing I'm getting. It's not just hard to see cos of the black. The face itself is black.

'Blade,' it says.

A low, slow voice.

'Come back to us, boy.'

I'm not coming back. I'm bloody staying here. And hanging round till I hook up with Death. He's got to get here soon. I just got to keep looking for him. The black gobbo's face has faded. Thank God for that. But now he's started talking again.

'You got to fight this, boy. You hear me? Biggest fight you ever had. Cos you hurt bad. You hurt real bad. So come on. Give us what you got.'

I'm not giving him anything. I'm staying put.

And when Death turns up, I'm diving straight in his bag. Wigging it out of here. All the way to nothing. Beautiful, beautiful nothing. You know why, Bigeyes? Cos I failed. Failed bad.

Didn't avenge Becky. Didn't kill Hawk.

And that little kid won't have done either. A knife dink in the back won't have nailed it. Hawk'll have turned round after shooting me and blown the kid's head off. I just wish he'd blown mine off too. I'd have been dead quicker.

But I'm almost there.

Just need a bit of quiet.

And I'll be gone.

But here's that gobbo's voice again. And now there's something strange. It sounds familiar. Why's that? Didn't sound familiar before. And I didn't recognize the face when I had it. Maybe it was too blurred. I just knew it wasn't one of the slugs I killed.

'Come on, boy,' says the voice. 'Don't give up.'

Yeah, I got it now. Who the guy is, I mean.

But he tells me anyway.

'It's Poppa,' he says. 'Becky's grandpa.'

Wish he hadn't said that. The last bit. He didn't need to. Just makes it worse. Hearing her name. Makes me want to die even more. It's not Poppa's fault, bless his heart. How's he to know how bad I failed? How I can't bear to face him? Or Becky's mum.

And Ruby's bound to be here with him.

I'm dreading hearing her voice.

But it's still Poppa doing the talking. Only something's changed suddenly. He's not speaking to me. He's speaking to someone else, and he's talking quick. And Poppa never talks quick.

'Doctor!' he's saying. 'He's going!'

Footsteps, another voice.

'Nurse, over here!'

And suddenly there's gabbling all around.

'We're losing him,' someone says.

I take no notice. Cos you know what? Suddenly the black's got deeper—and oh, you beauty, you're squeezing me away, squeezing out everything Blade ever was, and now he's gone and there's just this tiny little bit left.

A flickering spark of what I might have been. Too late to mend, too late to start again. And now that's going too. Thank Christ. Cos here's the gobbo I've been looking for. I knew he'd come. I knew he wouldn't let me down.

Death.

Sweet lovely Death. Come to take me away.

Yeah, big man. Close me up, pop me in your little bag. Let's go.

But we don't go. Cos suddenly there's words again. Only they're not like normal words. They're floating in the darkness like a frozen dream.

'Don't die for Becky.'

I feel a shudder. Cos it's not Death talking. It's another voice. A voice I'm even more scared of. There's a long silence. A long, black silence. Then Ruby speaks again.

'Live for Becky,' she says.

So I live. But it's a strange, dusky life. Cos everything's shadows right now. I'm not speaking. Can't speak. Don't know why. I want to. I want to say lots. I want to find out what happened.

But every time I open my mouth, nothing comes.

So I listen to everybody else.

And there's plenty of nebs to fizz onto. They're all naffing. Yak yak yak, all around me. Can't see 'em clear. Like I say, they're all shadows. And I can't hear 'em good either. Not the words, I mean. Just the yakky drone.

They're hospital nebs. I worked that out. But not much else. Except that I like 'em. Yeah, they're cool. They keep checking me over. One of 'em stroked my face, made a cooing noise. Felt good. And one time they rushed round, bustling. I can't remember what was wrong.

Something to do with me.

Cos I went blacko again.

But it wasn't scary. Not this time. I saw Becky's face in there. And it felt good. And somehow I knew Ruby was right. I knew I was going to come back. Eventually. And I did. I woke up. And the hand stroked my face again.

And so it's gone on. They've moved me a couple of times. Maybe more times than I know. Cos I keep sleeping. Can't stay awake, except when the pain kicks in. And someone rushes over. And it goes dark again.

But here's the thing, Bigeyes. I've kind of stopped worrying. I want to live for Becky. I've decided that. But you know what? If I don't make it, that's cool too. Cos then I'll get to meet her.

And how good would that be?

So now it's simple. Win and live, win and die.

Yeah, yeah. I know what you're thinking. You're thinking—win? Who's won what? Cos we still don't know what happened to Hawk. That's true, Bigeyes. Good point. But I'll tell you something. Something I worked out in this dreamy little world I'm in.

There's winning and there's winning.

And I know one thing. Whatever else I've done

wrong, I've done one or two things right. And you know what? I'm going to call that winning. Winning something back. Something I can give to Becky.

And make her forgive me.

Maybe even love me.

I've been thinking about that a lot. Love, I mean. Cos the thing is, I never dreamt Becky could possibly love me. That time I told you what I saw in her face, and Mary's face, and Jaz's face—remember what I called it?

The opposite of hate.

The thing that couldn't be love.

But why couldn't it be love? Eh? Cos here's something that's slammed me. Last time I saw Becky's face, when I was blacko, she wasn't like in that photo of Ruby's. Or even like in my memory. Cos in those pictures she's kind of a goddess. I look at her and think—how could she possibly love a claphead like me?

How could anyone?

But when I was blacko, she didn't look like that. She just looked at me like . . . like it's OK, like I'm OK, like I'm still her friend. Like . . . she maybe could love me.

Like she maybe always did.

The hand's stroking my face again. I try to look, try to see who it is. But it's just a shadow. A friendly shadow. Murmurs something. I go on thinking about Becky. The hand rests on my cheek, moves away.

And Becky stays. Warm in my heart.

More dreams, more pain. Time's gone somewhere. Wigged it. I don't know where. Got no idea how long I've been here. Or where I am. Yeah, yeah, some hospital. That's bung-clear. But don't ask me where it is.

I got a feeling I've been here several days. But I don't give two bells. Cos days have stopped being days now and it's like I'm floating through an endless night. Then suddenly it clears. I open my eyes and I don't see the dark.

I see sunlight pouring in through a window. I see a room with pale walls, artificial flowers, screens round part of the bed. Bleepy hospital gizmos. Shit painting on the far wall.

And Bex, sitting in a chair.

Watching my face.

I twist my head. It does what I want. Didn't expect it to. But it moves good. Cop a glint round. No other beds and nobody here. Just me and Bex. Sound of nursey voices down the corridor. I turn my head back, look at Bex.

She stands up, comes over, leans down.

'Can you see me?' she says.

Her voice is strange. The words sound clipped, like they never were with Bex. But maybe it's just me. I haven't heard proper words for a bit. She speaks again. And her voice sounds like it used to.

'Blade? Can you see me?'

'Yeah.'

'Jesus, you can talk!'

'Course I can bloody talk.'

'I'll go and get the others.'

'Wait.'

I try to reach out. But my arm feels heavy. She stays anyway.

'Take it easy,' she says.

'I'm all right.'

'You look like shit.'

'Piss off.'

She glances towards the corridor. I can tell she's thinking she's got to get help. Case I'm not right.

'I'm OK, Bex.'

'What?'

She's leaning close to hear. And I realize she's right. I must look like shit. Cos I still feel like shit. And just speaking those few words has worn me out. I'm probably talking softer than I thought.

I take a slow breath.

'Bex?'

'Yeah?'

'Before . . . before you get anybody . . . tell me what happened.'

She flicks another glance towards the corridor, then pulls her chair close, sits down, leans in.

'Can you hear me all right?' she says.

'Yeah, but . . . don't speak too fast.'

She talks slow.

'I don't know much, OK? About what happened. Police won't tell us. Just know my dad's been arrested. That's it. And you nearly died Christ knows how many times. You got shot to pieces. You know that, don't you? Doc says either you fought hard or you got lucky. Or it's just a miracle.'

I'll settle for the miracle, Bigeyes.

She leans closer.

'Ain't got much more to tell you. I ran away from my dad. And my bitch stepmother. Headed for Ruby's place. Found her there with a load of her mates. Big guy called Seth, three women, couple of other guys. You probably remember 'em. She said you was with 'em.'

'I remember. But what happened to 'em? I got . . .'

I feel the pain come back, and the weariness.

'Do you want to stop?' says Bex.

'No, listen . . .' I take another long breath. 'I got taken away, OK? By your dad's men.'

'I know about that bit. Ruby told me. She saw it out of the window of her house. My dad's a bastard. What did he do to you?'

'Never mind that. I got to know what happened to you? And Ruby and her mates?'

'Nothing. They was all OK. There was a bit of trouble with them guys what come looking for you. They roughed up Seth a bit. Threatened Ruby and the others. But nothing more. They all pissed off after you got took away.'

So it was that simple, Bigeyes. Jakes set the trap

and it was just for me. Thank Christ for that. Nobody else got shunted. And Bex is OK. I think. I look at her.

'Where you living now?'

'With Ruby.'

I relax. She'll be OK with Ruby. Ruby'll take care of her. Till Bex moves on. Which she will. Cos she always will. She's that kind of troll. Don't ask me how I know. Bex hesitates.

'Ruby told me about Jaz. What you done for her.'

She leans forward suddenly, kisses me on the cheek. Stands up quick.

'I'm getting the others,' she mutters.

But they're coming in anyway. Couple of nurses, a gobbo. I can tell he's the doc. Looks kind of young, but I like his face. And there's two more nebs. I feel a shiver run through me. A dronky kind of shiver.

Cos I'm happy and scared at the same time.

Ruby and Poppa.

They're standing back, letting the medics fiddle round. Nurses doing most of the fiddling, naffing at me quiet and friendly. How do they do that? Make like they're just talking to you casual but what they're really doing is checking you over.

The gobbo's doing his bit now. And he's naffing too. Talking to me like they are, the kind of talk that doesn't need an answer. And that's just as well cos I got nothing in me to answer anybody. Not right now.

That little bit of talking with Bex wiped me out.

'You don't need to answer,' says the doc.

Yeah, mate. Like I haven't worked that out.

They go on fiddling, checking pulse, blood pressure, whatever. Taking ages, and all the time I'm watching Ruby and Poppa. They're standing back, keeping out of the way, saying nothing. Just watching me.

Watching them.

Bex has sat down, but they're still standing. One of the nurses has pulled up a couple of free chairs for 'em, but they don't take 'em. They just stand there and watch. And I watch back. And it's like I said, Bigeyes.

I feel happy and scared seeing 'em.

Scared cos of the guilt. Yeah, I know. I probably shouldn't feel choked out. I mean, look at their faces. There's nothing in 'em that wants me to be frightened. Poppa looks just like he did the last time.

Old and sad and kind.

And Ruby?

Ruby looks . . .

Never mind. I guess I'm still scared of Ruby.

The doc's talking again, and this time he wants an answer.

'OK.' He looks hard at me. 'You can talk to your friends for just a few minutes. But I mean just a few. One of the nurses will come back and tell you when to stop. All right?'

I manage something with my eyes.

And he picks it up.

'Good.' He straightens up. 'We'll leave you to it. But take it easy. You'll find talking more tiring than you think.'

He looks round the room. And I can tell he's waiting for another answer. Ruby gives him a nod. And he picks that up too. A glance at the nurses and the medics wig it out the room.

Poppa and Ruby walk slowly up to the bed. Bex stands up and joins 'em. They stand there close by, all three of 'em, looking down at me. Then Poppa leans close, takes my hand, squeezes it gentle, speaks to me in that soft, slow voice.

'So have you stopped running now, son?'

I look up at him.

'Yeah, Poppa. I stopped running now.'

He's got tears in his eyes. Doesn't say any more. Just squeezes my hand again. I look up at Ruby. I so want her to speak. I want her to say something. Anything. Long as I can take it. But she doesn't speak. She just reaches out.

Rests a hand on my cheek.

I close my eyes. Cos suddenly I recognize that hand. It's the hand I felt before. When everything was dark. It wasn't one of the nurses. It was Ruby. Touching my face, murmuring. It was Ruby. Or maybe . . .

Maybe it was someone else.

I almost dare to think so.

So what do you know? Here we are again. Back at the old police station. Same room even. The one they shoved me in when I was seven and got jacked for stopping cars on the pedestrian crossing and swearing at the drivers.

Jesus, that was a gig.

Yeah, same old room. They might have done it up. But they've changed it a bit. The desk's different. And they got video kit in here for the interview. They didn't have that last time. Otherwise it's the same.

Apart from me being stuck in a wheelchair.

And getting blobbed with this gobbo from Social Services. They keep telling me I got to have him. For legal reasons. Can't be interviewed without him present. They say. I got nothing against him personal. I just don't need him.

I know how this works. I've been arrested and cautioned. I'm up for multiple murders. Now I'm going to get grilled. And I'm cute about that. I'm ready for what comes.

Apart from the journos outside. Wasn't quite ready for them. Or that many of 'em. I kind of forgot I'm big news. But never mind that. One thing at a time. Check round the room again.

Soggy Service guy's standing in the corner and there's a porker woman behind me. She's been pushing my wheelchair. Then there's the two porkers who came and got me from the hospital. Gloomy-looking gobbos.

Door opens and in comes DI Fern.

She's followed by Inspector Bannerman.

Jesus, Bigeyes. I wasn't expecting these two. Not him anyway.

They sit down behind the desk, fiddle with papers, keep their eyes away from mine. Bannerman gives a cough, glances up at the policewoman behind my wheelchair.

'We'll take care of that,' he says. 'Just move him a bit closer to the desk so the video picks him up.'

She eases me forward.

'That's fine,' says Bannerman.

She locks the wheels, then wigs it out the room. The two porker gobbos do the same. And now it's just four of us. Soggy pulls a chair up next to mine.

I glance at him, then turn to Bannerman.

'I don't need this guy.'

'He's required to be present,' says Bannerman. 'It's for your own support. He's simply here to observe proceedings and ensure that—'

'I know what he's here for. I just don't need him.'

I can see I'm getting nowhere. I bung a glance at Soggy.

'Don't take this the wrong way but . . . keep your mouth shut, OK?'

The guy shrugs. Doesn't answer. And that's cute with me. Long as he keeps that way. I turn back to Bannerman and Fern. They've started the video recorder and Bannerman's muttering the date and time and all the other gobbledyplonk. He finishes that and looks me in the eye.

I give him a wink.

'Got your old job back, Bannerman.'

'So it seems.'

'Like old times, then, yeah? Me sitting here, you sitting there. And Ferny.' I glance at her. 'Only you used to stand by the door.'

'I've been promoted,' she says.

I think that was a joke. But I'm not sure. I look back at Bannerman.

'So aren't you going to check?'

'Check what?' he says.

'That I haven't got a knife in my sock.'

'I'll take the risk.'

He's watching me hard. And I'm reading something in his face. It's not in Fern's, but it's in his. He's going through the procedure, yeah, doing what he's got to do, but his eyes are saying, let's cut the crap. You want to know stuff, I want to know stuff. Just give me what you got and I'll do the same.

Cos I'll tell you something, Bigeyes. He's reading my face too.

Reading it good.

'OK,' I say. 'No shit. You tell me what happened to you. I'll tell you what happened to me.'

He doesn't answer. But I know what he's thinking. He's thinking, how far can I go with this kid? Cos the thing is, Bigeyes, there's limits to what he can tell me. I know that. He can't say much about Jakes, for example—if anything—cos the bastard's been arrested and there's a separate investigation going on.

And we got a video rolling and Fern sitting there all proper and official, and Soggy making sure everything's done cute. So Bannerman's got to follow the script. But he also knows he's got to tell me something. If I'm going to talk too.

'Come on, Bannerman,' I murmur. 'I know the tricks. So forget the usual crap. You tell me your bit. As much as you want. And I'll tell you my bit.' I pause. 'As much as I want.'

He raises an eyebrow. Fern looks disapproving. The video goes on rolling. I lean forward, far as I can in the wheelchair.

'Listen, Bannerman, here's the thing. I wrote those lists out for you, remember?'

'I remember.'

'Well, they weren't just to help you clean up scum. They were also my confession. For the murders I did. I gave you all the names, wrote 'em out clear. Didn't miss a single one. So you got 'em all. Every dreg I ever killed. And I'm not denying any of 'em. I'm pleading guilty to all the murders on that list.'

'And what about the other murder?' says Fern quietly.

There's a silence.

'Lord Haffler-Devereaux,' says Bannerman.

I take a slow breath, lean back in the wheelchair again.

Lord Haffler-Devereaux. Yeah, Bigeyes. He died after all.

Thank Christ.

But nobody's going to tell me any more about it here. And I know why. Cos they're hoping I'm going to tell them. That's what this cosy chat's really about.

I think of that little boy. The tiny frightened kid who looked like me, could have been me. The seven-year-old me. I've been thinking about him a lot, Bigeyes. Wondering what happened to him.

And if he's still alive.

Nobody's mentioned him yet. So I won't either. I got to play this cute. I see Fern and Bannerman watching me. Waiting for what I got. I shake my head.

'You first,' I mutter. 'Then I'll talk.'

Bannerman frowns, glances at Fern, takes the plunge.

'You gave me those lists,' he says, 'and they were very helpful. But you also told me where I could find a backup hard drive from Lord Haffler-Devereaux's computer.'

He pauses, still frowning, then goes on.

'I put down the phone after speaking to you, drove through the night and dug it up.'

'But it did no good,' I cut in. 'Cos you just gave it to Jakes. And he smashed it up. I saw him do it.'

Bannerman rolls his eyes.

'Do you think I'm completely stupid?'

'Only sometimes.'

'I drove to DI Fern's on the way back. She copied all the material and I handed in the drive to my superior in the morning, together with the lists you gave me. I took copies of those too and gave them to DI Fern. During the day when I was suspended, DI Fern went through the computer files.'

OK, Bigeyes, I got it. And I'm starting to see the whole thing. Bannerman played it good, no question. Covered himself so even when Jakes blasted him, he could kick back. What I don't get is why it took Fern so long to smack the files on that backup drive.

The whole of the next day at least.

Cos that was the day I got caught and beaten up. If she'd splashed the stuff out quicker, Jakes might have got taken sooner and I might never have got snagged. But I guess I was meant to. Cos otherwise I might never have gone after Hawk.

Even so . . .

I look at Fern. She's still got that official face. I

won't get much out of her. But I'll give it a go. She might just tell me.

'What was on the backup drive?' I go.

She presses her lips together. Yeah, OK. She's not going to tell me anything. But then suddenly she answers.

'There were hundreds and hundreds of files,' she says. 'Every imaginable type. It was just as well you gave us the passwords. But it still took me the whole day and much of the evening to go through the material. And I'd almost given up hope of finding anything. Ninety-nine per cent of the files were completely above board. But then right at the end I found the few that weren't.'

She narrows her eyes.

'And they were dynamite.'

She doesn't say any more, but she doesn't need to. I've worked out the rest. By the time she got to the end of those files, I was halfway to Hawk's nest. She probably shared what she had with someone in authority, someone she could trust.

And the porkers got cracking.

Pulled in Jakes. I'm guessing Fern found his name

in one of those files. Jakes blotches on Hawk to help his own case, squeals on where the nest is. Bannerman's brought back into the fold and they all blast off.

And now I'm thinking of those last moments in Hawk's tower. When I was lying on my back and heard shouts outside the door. I'd already heard motors, remember? A convoy of 'em. And Hawk said they were backup. Well, maybe they were.

But not for him.

I'm guessing it was Bannerman and the porkers storming in.

'You found me in the tower,' I say. 'Lying there, shot, right?'

Bannerman nods. I feel Soggy shift on his chair. I glance at him. He says nothing, just watches. I think of the little boy again. Look back at Bannerman and Fern.

And start to talk.

I tell 'em what happened. Or most of what happened. Trying to jump off Bogeybum Bridge, Ruby rescuing me, taking me back to Poppa's, getting caught by Jakes, handed over to Hawk's grinks.

Getting beaten up, getting away.

Picking up the bomb vest. I don't say who from.

And they don't ask.

The video goes on rolling.

I tell 'em about driving to Hawk's nest, watching the house, climbing up the wall, breaking in to the tower. Hawk coming in, watching the stars. Turning to face me. And then I stop.

Cos I can't tell 'em more. Without them telling me more.

The silence feels heavy, strained. Bannerman speaks suddenly.

'There's something that's not right,' he says.

'What's that?'

He looks at me.

'You went in there, risking all, strapped inside a bomb vest. We're not here to question your motivation for suicide. But if murder was your other intention, as seems to be the case, I would have thought that the bomb vest on its own would have been sufficient to kill both you and your enemy.'

Bannerman leans forward on the desk.

'So why with such a weapon at your disposal did you bother to stab Lord Haffler-Devereaux repeatedly

in the back? And so very messily. The coroner noted
that the stab wounds were amateurish. They weren't
accurate, they weren't deep. They were just messy. It's
hardly the work of a practised assassin. And how did
you manage it anyway? Since he clearly had a gun and
used it on you.'

I feel a shudder run through me.

Repeatedly? Stabbed repeatedly?

I think of the boy again. That tiny little kid. Did he
do that? Did he really do that? I hope he got away.
Trouble is, even if he did, what did he get away to?
What kind of a future? I think of what I was, Bigeyes.
What I've become. What I want to be. What I desper-
ately want to be.

Something else.

Something better.

I turn my face to the video camera.

'I killed Lord Haffler-Devereaux. I did it cos of all
the stuff he did to me. I was going to just blow us both
up. But I couldn't help myself. He started mocking me
so I whipped a knife into his back. He went down but
I kept on stabbing him. I just couldn't stop, even after
I thought he was dead. I hated him so much. That's

why I made a mess of it. I wasn't thinking straight. But then I kind of calmed down and stopped and turned away. But he must have still been alive cos he plugged me with his gun. But I don't remember any of that. I just went unconscious.'

I look away. Can't face the video camera.

It's easier to lie to Bannerman.

But I don't think he believes me either.

'So what did you do with the knife?' he says.

I'm still looking away. Can't face any of 'em now. Not even Bannerman. All I can look at is the picture in my head of that little boy. Holding a hunting knife he never should have picked up.

'I got rid of it, Pugface,' I say.

Soggy speaks for the first time.

'Pugface?'

I look round at him.

'My pet name for Inspector Bannerman.'

I glance over at Fern.

'I got one for you too. But I don't reckon you want to hear it.'

She doesn't answer. Just asks another question.

'Are you really asking us to believe that you got rid

of the knife in the brief moment between stabbing Lord Haffler-Devereaux and getting shot?'

'Yeah.'

'Don't you think that's something of an achievement?'

I look down at the floor.

'Nothing to it,' I whisper.

Yeah, Bigeyes.

Nothing to it.

And all that happened was when I was fourteen.

Yeah, Bigeyes. Long time ago.

Now that I've turned twenty-one, I look back and you know what's weird? It's like nothing's changed. I still don't like the police and I still don't like people getting close.

But it's not as bad as it was when I was a kid.

Cos to be honest with you, there was nobody I liked back then. Apart from sweet Becky of course. Yeah, right. I'm zipping you over. I'm not being honest. Truth is, I wasn't looking out for friends in those days. I was looking out for grime.

Cos that's all I'd ever known.

But since that time I've found lots of nebs to care for. And some of 'em even care for me. For all the crap I've done. I didn't use to believe it. But I do now. Feels kind of good. To be cared for, I mean. So I guess that's one crack up the line.

And there's another thing.

Prison's OK.

It's rough but it's OK. You got to see the shit coming and long as you do that, you got options. Blast out or blast back. Whatever works. I got a name goes with me so I'm there for the slam. And some of 'em try it.

So I got to watch cute all the time, right?

First place they put me in was for young kids. They didn't call it prison. They called it 'secure accommodation'. Yeah, right. It's a prison, OK? Good nebs running it. No claphead officers. And they treated me fair, no question.

The other kids weren't too friendly but once the crap died down about who I was and how I fitted in, things got better and it was almost like being in a snug. Better than a snug really. Cos in a snug you're always on your own. But in prison you get something else.

You get help.

I got given this counsellor gobbo called Dominic, and we talk regular, which is good, cos I like him. And I need it. Talking, I mean. To straighten me out a bit, make sense of the flashbacks and nightmares. And there's a priest called Father Brendan. I like him too. And there's nebs from Soggy Services, and mentors and stuff.

And then there's something else.

There's books.

Yeah, Bigeyes, books.

I started reading Day One. Pretty soon I'd read everything they had in the prison library so they had to get more books in for me. And then I started doing something Becky always wanted me to do.

Getting educated.

Yeah, that's right. Doing lessons. Cos they got all that bung organized in these places. You got to be up for it, but if you are, they fix you up with tutors. It's great. You can learn as much as you want. They're big time into that. You learning, I mean.

And there's one thing I learned straight up.

Well, two things.

First, Becky was right. It's fun. And second, it's a whack. I'm telling you, Bigeyes, the stuff they give kids in schools is a jink. Well, it is for me anyway. End of the first year they'd run out of things I couldn't do.

So they got me taking exams.

Whacked on through those, bang bang bang, nothing to 'em, and I get to like fifteen, sixteen years old, and I'm taking stuff they do at university. Year or two later I'm through that.

They move me on to another prison. For young offenders. Same again. Just a different name. And older kids having a pop at me. Anyway, I keep on studying. And it's just the same.

Nothing to it. They kept trying to find subjects that weren't easy piss for me. But everything was easy piss. So they gave me these intelligence tests. High level stuff, you know? The tests they give the really nerdy nobs.

And I kind of freaked everybody out with the results.

Cos I was pretty much off the scale.

That's when they started making special arrangements for me. The prison nebs, I mean. To keep me fizzing along. Can't say they haven't bent over backwards for me. Cos they have. They've been brilliant. They already had me massive into distance learning. Now they fixed up for me to see these special tutors.

You know, brainboxes.

Like the Maths guy. Clever Trevor, I call him. Yeah, I know. Not very original. Anyway, he's mega into Maths, this dronk. And I mean serious, spooky Maths. He's on another planet, reality-wise, but he's wired into Maths.

And I really hooked on with him.

Total disaster as a human being. No social skills and a voice like a farting balloon, but I don't give two bells. His lessons are a blitz. He just starts talking about numbers and every time he takes me to a new place.

And there's other tutors they brought in special.

I won't mention 'em all.

Except Dorothea. Can't leave her out. Retired professor, super bloody bright, keeps losing her pen. We started going through literature and history and philosophy and stuff. She couldn't believe I can read a book in an hour. Proper, I mean. But once I'd done a few books and shown her I got what was in 'em, we were cool.

And we still are.

She's not stuffy. Got a brain like a bee. We'll be talking about Jane Austen or Shakespeare or whatever and she'll suddenly go, 'Did you know Napoleon found it hard to sit on his horse at Waterloo because he was suffering from piles?'

So yeah, Bigeyes. Prison's OK.

Long as I watch my back.

And now they moved me to this new one. With the grown-up dronks. I guess it means I've grown up too. But you know what? Same again. I keep my nose clean, give no trouble. And on the whole I get none back.

Thing is, in prison, you got to act smart. Got to know when to talk, when to say nothing. And when you do talk, you got to say it right. It's all about respect here. If you got that, you get a quiet life.

And that's all I want now, Bigeyes.

That and books.

And the nebs I just told you about.

And the visitors.

Yeah, Bigeyes. I get visitors too.

Bannerman comes in. We get on good now. I guess we always did. He's left the porkers. Says he wants to devote more time to his drinking. I don't ever see Fern. I think they split up. If they were ever together. And here's something plum.

Jaz is doing fine. Bannerman told me last time I saw him. Said he'd made a few enquiries cos he knew I care. I had to look away, Bigeyes. I don't mind admitting it. Cos I think about Jaz a lot. Can't quite believe she'll be close on eleven.

Same age Becky was when she died.

Anyway . . .

Bex used to come in but she's kind of faded. Got a boyfriend now, I think, and last time she came in she said they were moving in together. But that was a couple of years ago. Haven't heard from her since.

Ruby's the opposite. Bless her heart. Hasn't missed a visit—ever. Poppa came with her too, right up to the week he died. I thought maybe Ruby would stop after that, specially since she told me she's got a guy now.

But she still never misses a visit, even though it costs her a pile of jippy. And she gave me something special. Check this out.

Photo of Becky.

Same photo Ruby's got on her little shrine at home, only smaller. Which is cute, cos I can carry it about with me. And I do. You better believe it. Only time it comes out of my pocket is when I want to look at it.

Or at night. When it goes under my pillow.

So that's my life here, Bigeyes. I read, study, see people. Keep busy, keep smart, keep out of trouble. And think. Yeah, I think a lot. And there's one other thing. Something I started doing recently.

Using a knife.

But not in the old way. Come over here, Bigeyes. Check out the shelf.

Three sculptures.

Carved out of wood. With a good old-fashioned blade.

We got this instructor called Arty. Teaches painting and pottery and joinery and stuff in the prison workshop. He's careful who he trusts with the tools. But he seems to be cute with me.

So now I'm back with the knife. And I got to tell you, Bigeyes, it felt strange first time I held it after so many years. But you know what? Moment I started carving, something took over. It was like my hands weren't mine any more.

Just like in the old days. When I used the knife for bad shit. My hands just moved by themselves. And here I found the same thing. But this time it wasn't for bad shit.

It was for something good, something worth doing.

Go on, Bigeyes. Cop a glint. Look close. What do you see? Come on, Bigeyes. You got to see it. Arty says I'm good, says I could be amazing if I keep at it. So surely you must see what these sculptures are?

OK. Yeah, yeah. You got it now. Left to right.

Becky, Mary, Jaz.

Three angels.

Carved out of wood.

Then I get a new visitor.

No one tells me he's coming or who he is. They just

take me through and there he is, sitting in the visit room, waiting. Old gobbo, ancient even. Must be over eighty. I know him straight up.

Only ever saw him once, and that was seven years ago. He was standing by a window, looking out as I ran by. But I'd have recognized him anyway. It's in the face. The mouth, the cheeks, the green eyes. Specially them.

And that other thing. The thing with no name. The thing they all got, the people I love. And she had it. Oh, yeah. You bet.

'You're Mary's brother,' I say. 'You're Jacob.'

He doesn't answer. Just studies me, quiet, slow. He's a bit like Poppa, this gobbo. Takes his time. Got plenty of spit too, like Mary. No question. I can tell. I like him.

Not sure he likes me. He's still checking me close. I wait, take my time too. He goes on watching me, then leans slowly forward.

'Yes, I'm Jacob.'

And there's that dreamy Irish voice. Like music.

He's still not sure of me. I got a feeling he didn't want to come. Which case he's doing this for someone else. And there's only one person that could be. I think of her. Like I so often do. Last time I saw her I told her I love her.

And I meant it.

'Mary was my friend,' I say.

I fix Jacob in the eyes.

'And she always will be.'

His face doesn't move. But something changes in it. Just a small thing. And I know I scored a point.

'She saved my life twice,' I say.

'I know.' He pauses. 'And you tried to save hers by driving to The Crown to warn her when you thought she was in danger. And nearly got yourself killed doing so. I saw it from the window.'

He falls silent.

But I think I scored another point.

He turns away suddenly and coughs. A rough, rasping cough. Doesn't sound good. And when he turns back, I see something else in his face. Something I didn't notice before. I think of Mary and her cancer.

'Yes,' he says quietly. 'I'm not doing so well.'

His eyes tell me not to push this further.

'Can you tell me about Mary?' I say. 'Last I heard she was in a hospice.'

'She died there. Quite peaceful. I was with her right through.'

Jacob coughs again, then goes on.

'They looked after her well. She had no regrets. She was even serene at the end.'

He looks down.

'And it's partly because of you.'

He falls silent again. And I can tell he's struggling inside. Cos he's still not sure of me. And who's to blame him, Bigeyes? Eh? I wouldn't be sure of me if I was him.

I think of Mary.

Beautiful Mary. Brave Mary.

Yeah, brave as you'll ever get.

Remember what she said about getting kidnapped and tortured? All cos of her bitch sister. And then breaking out and running for it. Jesus, she was some woman. Braver than I've ever been. Braver than any of the guys in this prison. And there's some hard dronks in here.

I'm glad she died sweet.

Back in the old city.

Jacob looks up again.

'She talked about you a lot,' he says. 'She worried about you.'

'I didn't want her worrying about me.'

'Neither did I.'

I feel the edge in his voice and look away. A picture floats into my head, of Mary last time I saw her. She was lying in that dronky bed. Weak and ill but full of spirit. I hate to think of her worrying about me when she was dying.

Jacob speaks again.

Like he's picked up my thought.

'She wasn't worrying about you right at the end. Because by then she'd made a decision. And talked me round to it. Which took some doing, I have to admit.'

We fix eyes again.

He goes on, slow.

'Have you given any thought to what you'll do if they ever let you out of here?'

I shrug.

'They won't.'

'You don't know that.'

'Yeah, I do,' I say. 'I'm here for good. And fair enough. I don't deserve to be outside. I'm a danger to society. You got any idea how many guys I killed?'

'I know exactly how many guys you killed. I also know you're no danger to anyone.'

Jacob holds my gaze.

'And I know other things about you too.'

He frowns.

'But I only found out what I really needed to know in the last few minutes.'

He leans back in the chair, still watching me. And for a moment I see Mary's eyes in his, watching me too.

'You might be right,' he says eventually. 'They may never let you out of prison. But I also think it's possible that in ten, twenty, thirty years, whatever, you may find yourself outside with a new name, a new identity and a new start.'

'You got some special information I don't know about?'

Jacob shakes his head.

'I just think it's possible that some years from now they'll give you another chance.'

'Why should they?'

'Because you deserve another chance.'

I watch him close. There was something in that last sentence.

Something he's still fighting. I felt it in the words.

'You don't believe that,' I say.

He doesn't answer. I try again.

'You don't believe I deserve another chance. Not really. You're here cos someone else believed it. Someone special to both of us. And you made a promise to her. And now you're worried you won't be able to honour that promise cos you're ill, cos you're . . .'

I stop. Don't want to say it. But he nods.

'You're right,' he says. 'And you're also wrong.'

He turns away, gives another rasping cough, looks back.

'You're right that it was Mary who believed in you and not me. Even while I was sitting here waiting for you, I didn't want to see you. But I made a promise to Mary, and yes, I'm not going to be around much longer, and I couldn't bear the thought of dying without doing what I told her I would.'

He gives another cough.

'But you're also wrong. Because in the last few minutes I've seen what she saw in you.'

I stare at him.

'But I haven't done anything in the last few minutes. Haven't said anything. Nothing special anyway.'

'It's not about that,' says Jacob. 'It's about . . . just knowing. Knowing when something's right.'

He pauses.

'And I've got a feeling you understand exactly what I mean by that.'

I do, Bigeyes. Christ, I do.

But I say nothing.

He reaches down suddenly, pulls a sheet of paper out of a bag, pushes it over to me. I look down at it. It's a page torn from a recipe book. There's a heading with the words 'Coq au Vin', then a list of ingredients and a description of how to cook it.

I bung a glance at Jacob.

And catch another new thing in his face. The nearest thing I've seen to a smile.

'Other side,' he murmurs.

I turn the page over.

'Mary tore it out of a recipe book at The Crown,' he adds. 'It was all we could find in a hurry.'

And there on the other side is what was once a blank page. Only now it's been covered by a blotty red pen. Handwritten words at the top. Mary's name, address, date of birth, other stuff about her. Then underneath that a heading in capital letters.

BLADE.

And then a written description of what I'm like. Or what I was like when I was fourteen. When I last saw Mary. She's described my face, my hair, everything she can think of. And then she's done a drawing. Or more like a diagram.

And I shudder.

Cos I recognize right away what it is.

She's drawn the wounds on my back. The knife marks I showed her that night in The Crown. Drawn 'em spot on. No wonder she got Jacob to tear a sheet out quick, first thing they could find. She'd want to draw the wounds while she had 'em in her mind.

I look up at Jacob.

'Why this?' I ask.

'She knew so little about you,' he says, 'and she wanted to describe you in as much detail as she could. Because she wanted this paper to be a legal document. Something that could be used to identify both her and you. That's why she signed and dated it at the bottom and had it witnessed by myself and one of the nurses at the hospice.'

He stares down at the paper.

'You're a young man,' he murmurs. 'To someone my age you're a young man. And in ten or twenty or even thirty years, you'll still be a young man. You'll still have a future.'

Another silence.

I swear I hear my heart beating.

Jacob looks up, leans closer.

'During Mary's last few days,' he says, 'she added an expression of wishes to her will. It was something she wanted me to honour. I didn't want to promise it. Certainly not without a stack of conditions. But she wouldn't have it. There were to be no conditions of any kind. All she said to me was . . .'

He lowers his voice.

'Leave the farm to Blade.'

The knife darts forward. Flick, twist, jab. It has no thinking behind it. The knife hates thoughts. Thoughts freeze it. So it moves like it's always moved. In its own space. With its own life. And I just watch.

Flick, twist, jab.

Chip, chip, chip.

The block of wood starts to change.

I look round the prison workshop. Just three other inmates. Matti and Tex doing paintings, Dosh trying another pot. He stuffed up the last two. Arty's supervising from the far end. But he looks cool.

Cos none of us is trouble.

Chip, chip, chip.

I turn the block, look it over.

Chip, chip, chip.

Don't know what to feel, Bigeyes. I guess I'm blown away.

Mary, Mary.

I can't believe she did it. And no conditions. Her farm in southern Ireland. Jacob says it's mine the moment he passes away. He's got it sorted, legal-wise. Says there's no complications. Mary's sister Louisa's died. So's her husband.

And the farm's being run by three gobbos Mary used to employ. Close friends of hers. Father and two sons. Honest guys, Jacob says. They know about Mary's last wish and they're going to stay on after Jacob dies. For her sake and his.

And the farm's going to be held in trust for me.

Yeah, Bigeyes.

Trust.

Good word.

Something it's taken me a long time to understand. Jaz used to trust. Remember that time Bex said to me, 'She just trusts,' and I thought how stupid? Cos I reckoned everybody who trusts must be stupid. But that's only cos I didn't know how to trust.

So Jaz taught me. Like Becky did.

And now Mary's done the same.

Jacob says I can do what I like with the farm. Sell it or work it. But I could see the challenge in his face when he said that. And I could feel the word coming at me again through his eyes.

Trust.

Yeah, Bigeyes.

All the way from Mary.

And I'm telling you, I won't betray that trust. If I'm stuck in prison for life, fair enough. I'll crack it best I can. But if I ever get out, I'll make that farm work. I'll do everything I can to persuade those three gobbos to stay on. And teach me what I got to know. They just might come to trust me too. If I can show 'em I learn quick.

And that's one thing I am sure about.

I learn quick.

Chip, chip, chip.

Turn the block, look it over.

Chip, chip, chip.

Got so many emotions running through me, Bigeyes. I never thought I had a future. Didn't reckon I deserved one. Not outside anyway. And maybe it's pie in the sky. Maybe I'm here for good. But even if I never see the farm, I got something else.

Hope.

Cos that's what Mary's really given me.

'Shit!' comes a shout.

I look up from the block of wood. Dosh has screwed up another pot. He's glumming down at the mess. Tex leans round the side of his painting, calls over to him.

'Looks good from here, man.'

'Piss off!'

Tex dissolves. Matti flicks paint at him. I see Arty coming over. He trigs up, stops by me.

'How you doing?' he says.

'OK.'

Chip, chip, chip.

I feel him staring at the block of wood.

'Your wife had her baby yet?' I mutter.

'Not last time I looked.'

Chip, chip, chip.

'What you working on?' he says.

'Come back later.'

He chuckles and trigs back to the others.

Yeah, yeah. So what am I working on, Bigeyes?

More than Arty knows, more than I know. I guess I'm just working on . . . making sense of all this. Cos it still doesn't seem possible they could ever let me out. But Jacob's right about one thing.

I'm no danger to anyone. Haven't been for a very long time. And never will be again. And I guess they know that in here. Cos here's something, Bigeyes. I never wanted to touch a knife again, right? Never went near one in prison.

Till someone stuck a blade in my hand.

Know who that was?

Arty.

He stood next to me, like he did just now, and said go on, mate, try making a sculpture. Here's a block of wood. And then he hands me a knife. And just turns away. Lets me get on with it.

Trust.

Yeah, again.

Chip, chip, chip.

So who's left to hate? Not Hawk. And I don't just mean cos he's dead. I don't hate him anyway. Or his slimehead friends. International porkers cleaned up some of those bastards. I heard it on the news.

Raven, Swift, Condor, some of 'em. Not all. And not Eagle. The Number One. Eagle's still out there. Whoever Eagle is. I just know they haven't nailed that dreg.

So the Game's still alive.

But I'm no part of it any more. I got no further role to play.

Thank Christ.

So yeah, who's left to hate? Hard to say now cos I'm running out of enemies. But there is one left, Bigeyes. One enemy I got to sort. I turn the block of wood again, check it over.

Chip, smooth, brush away the shavings.

Hold it up.

Sound of goony laughter, then footsteps. I look up. They're coming over, all four of 'em.

'What you got, then?' says Matti.

They crowd round, jostling. Only Arty stands back a bit.

Got a quiet smile on his face. And is that just coincidence?

Cos Mary had a smile like that.

'What you got, then?' says Matti again.

I hold up the sculpture, turn the head round so they see the face. They study it gravely.

'That you as a kid?' says Matti eventually.

Dosh sniffs.

'Man, you was one ugly shit.'

'My dog looked better than you,' says Tex. 'And that was when I buried him.'

I cuff him round the head.

Arty leans in, raises my arm so the sculpture moves close to my face. Then gives a nod.

'Good likeness,' he says. 'Even allowing for the difference in age. How old are you meant to be in this sculpture? Six, seven, eight?'

'Seven.'

'That's very precise.'

'Yeah, it is.'

They don't ask any more. But they go on looking.

And not seeing.

I'm glad they don't see. They aren't meant to. Nobody's meant to. I don't want anyone to see who this figure really is. And I don't think anyone ever will. I know it looks like me when I was seven. But it's not me. It's the little boy.

The boy who killed my enemy.

And then disappeared.

I'll never forget him, Bigeyes. And now I got him carved in wood so he can sit there with Becky and Mary and Jaz.

Cos he's an angel too.

The guys break off, back to their work. And I break off, back to my thoughts.

Cos I still haven't answered the question.

Who's left to hate?

Truth is, Bigeyes, there's no one. But like I said earlier, I still got one enemy to sort. I don't hate him, but I want to nail him. Cos he's tough and gritty and clever and he won't go away. Unless I deal with him. So yeah. Just one big enemy left.

ME.

Night. Prison's quiet. I love this time. I like the days cos I keep busy and I'm happy being busy, but I like the nights even better. Nights are when I lie awake in my little cell and gaze up, and dream.

Check that out, Bigeyes. The ceiling. All dark and still.

But it's not really a ceiling. Not right now. Right now it's a big glass dome, like Hawk had in his tower, and I'm peering through it at the night sky. And it's a big clear sky. Jesus, it's so clear.

Not a cloud anywhere and stars popping out all

over it. And the funnyface moon glinting down.

Remember that night I spent shivering in a pipe on that building site? I looked up and saw Orion sparkling down at me. I got an even better view from here. Check over the sky, Bigeyes. You name the star, I'll point it out.

I know where they all are.

I learnt 'em.

And now I got 'em. Safe in my head.

Close my eyes, take a slow breath.

Yeah, Bigeyes. I am the last enemy. I'm everything that stands in the way of being the person I should be. I got help everywhere I look. I got Ruby and Bannerman and Dorothea and Trevor and Arty and Dominic and Father Brendan and Jacob, and all kinds of other nebs behind me.

And I got my angels to inspire me.

But the past still slams in. The flashbacks and nightmares keep coming. I hoped they might ease up but they don't. Father Brendan says they probably never will go. Not total. I got to accept 'em, he reckons. He also says I got to forgive myself.

I know he's right. Cos there's someone in the way. And that person's me. I want to nail that last enemy. I want to forgive him. But I need your help, Bigeyes. Cos I can't do this on my own.

Open my eyes. Look over at the shelf.

My angels sit quietly watching. Reach under my pillow, pull out Becky's photo, hold it close, look up at the dream sky, the dream moon, the dream stars.

Think back, Bigeyes. Right back.

Cos I got a question for you.

How come I only started talking to you when I was fourteen? Eh? Cos I didn't before that. I didn't even know you were there. I just . . . crashed through my life and messed up and . . . never even knew about you.

Till I was fourteen.

So what happened when I was fourteen? Did you come looking for me? Cos I don't remember looking for you. Maybe we came looking for each other. Without even knowing it.

But I'll tell you something, Bigeyes.

First time we talked I said I didn't like people getting close, remember? And I said that included you. Well, it did back then. I wasn't ready to talk. Not even to you. But now? I'm glad you're there, Bigeyes. I really am. I'm glad I can talk to you. I just wanted to tell you that.

Not that you don't still piss me off sometimes. Even after all these years. Specially when I screw up something. Cos that's the time when I don't want anyone knowing what I've done. And there you are, gawping at me.

I hated that in the beginning. I wanted you around, yeah. But only on my terms. It's different now, honest. Cos here's something I've learned. About you seeing everything.

That's your strength. And if I can just deal with it, then it's my strength too. Not worrying about you knowing. Good or bad, no bum gripe. Cos there's another strength you got. And I really like this one.

You don't judge me.

I wish I had that strength but I don't. I judge all the time. I can feel myself doing it. Dosh splats up his pot and I'm thinking what a dimp. How difficult can it be to make a pot? And then I feel you watching me. Not judging, just watching.

And I kind of learn something myself. About watching, not judging.

So why? Eh, Bigeyes? Why didn't we meet earlier? You know what I think? I think we were meant to meet but I had to be ready. Simple as that. I had to be ready. And I was. Took me till I was fourteen, but I got there in the end.

Maybe I'm right, maybe I'm wrong.

But there's one thing I am clear about.

We're never going to be apart, Bigeyes. No messing. You and me. We're in this together. For good. Don't ask me how I know. But I'm cool about it. Oh, yeah. I wouldn't want it any other way.

Cos I can't imagine a life now without you in it.

I kiss Becky's photo. Look at my angels.

Look at the night sky.

Makes me think of that bit in *The Wind in the Willows*. When Ratty and Mole go off in their boat under the moonlight. They've heard their mate Otter's little kid's gone missing so they go looking for him. They row down the river towards this island, cos they got a feeling he might be somewhere there.

And as they get close, the dawn starts breaking. And they hear this soft music in the air. And they're kind of scared and excited at the same time. Cos they know there's something strange and mysterious and beautiful close by. They can feel it but they don't know what it is. But they row on and moor the boat and trig off over the island.

And find the little otter fast asleep.

And then they have this vision.

Of a big friendly spirit watching over 'em.

Right there, on the island.

And everything's plum, Bigeyes. They're scared and confused and they feel weak and vulnerable, but everything's plum. I used to dream of that vision. In my snugs, when I was curled up on someone else's bed, trying to sleep, I used to pretend I was the little otter, lying there.

With a big friendly spirit watching over me.

And dawn breaking.

I kiss Becky's photo again.

I'll settle for what I got, Bigeyes.

My memories, my angels, my future.

My big friendly spirit.

My dawn breaking.

And you. Sweet friend.

I'll settle for you.

Tim Bowler is one of the UK's most compelling and original writers for teenagers. He was born in Leigh-on-Sea and after studying Swedish at university, he worked in forestry, the timber trade, teaching and translating before becoming a full-time writer. He lives with his wife in a small village in Devon and his workroom is an old stone outhouse known to friends as 'Tim's Bolthole'.

Tim has written seventeen books and won fifteen awards, including the prestigious Carnegie Medal for *River Boy*. His most recent novel is the gripping *Bloodchild* and his provocative *BLADE* series is being hailed as a groundbreaking work of fiction. He has been described by the *Sunday Telegraph* as 'the master of the psychological thriller' and by the *Independent* as 'one of the truly individual voices in British teenage fiction'.

'Nobody in children's writing is producing anything like this.'
    Jill Murphy, *Bookbag*

Read the other titles in this compelling series

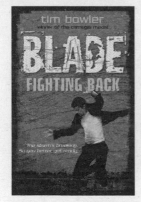

The body was lying in a thicket – a woman of about thirty – and Maya wouldn't have noticed it at all if she hadn't tripped over a root and rolled up against it. She scrambled back to her feet and stared down. The figure lay motionless, dusk settling over it. From a distant part of the forest came the sound of Tom calling.

'Maya!'

'Tom!' she called back.

But she knew he couldn't hear her. She'd

shouted repeatedly but his voice had continued to move further from her. He was clearly heading back to the village. He tried once more, even so.

'Where are you?'

That was the trouble. She didn't know. She didn't even remember how she'd ended up here. Something must have made her run away from Tom and cut into the trees, yet her mind was a shadow. She had a ghost of recollection.

Something on the path, something yellow.

But that was all.

She didn't shout back this time. She knew there was no point; and besides, she now had a bigger problem. She looked down at the body. She had to check this out, however scared she felt. There was just a chance this woman was alive. She took a slow breath, then knelt down.

The ground felt hard and bony. She peered at the body, wary in case it suddenly moved, but all was still. She inched nearer, the dusk thickening around her. Even this close it was hard to make out the figure clearly, but gradually the image defined itself.

A curvy form, chest and stomach still, so too the face. Eyes shut. A blue dress, the colour just discernible in the fading light, and a low neckline.

The woman seemed to have come from a party. There was no sign of an injury.

Something glinted in the darkness, a pendant nestling in the woman's cleavage: a horseshoe emblem on a slender chain. A lock of hair fell over it and then was still. Maya clenched her fists. This woman was surely dead.

And yet. . . .

'Are you alive?' she said.

Her voice sounded small in the darkening forest. There was no response, but from somewhere near came a rustling sound. She whirled round and peered into the gloom. The rustling stopped and silence fell once more.

She could feel herself starting to panic. She thought of her mobile back at home. Not that it would help much here. She had no idea how to describe where she was. She'd barely found her way round Hembury village in the few days since the family moved here. The forest she didn't know at all.

The rustling came again.

Then faded as before.

She stood up. She had to find the path home, raise the alarm, and somehow memorize the way to this place, so that she could describe it to the police. She looked about her and straightaway found the perfect marker: a huge beech tree, clearly damaged. Even in this poor light she could see that two of the lower branches had been cut off and a third was supported by a cradle of ropes from above.

She looked back at the body on the ground.

'I'm going to run back home,' she whispered. She had no idea why she was talking to this woman. 'I'm going to find Mum and Dad, and they'll call the police. I'll run as fast as I can. You won't be on your own for long.'

It was then that she heard footsteps.

Not heavy. Quite the opposite. They sounded stealthy. She crouched, her eyes moving fast. This didn't have to be dangerous. It might even be someone who could help, someone who might miss all this and walk straight past if she didn't call out or show herself.

But she stayed where she was and said nothing.

The footsteps drew closer. She edged behind an oak tree and waited. Closer, closer, slow footsteps – then suddenly they stopped and silence fell once more. She stayed behind the oak, her ears straining.

But all she heard was a rustle in the leaves

above her that died as she craned her head round to look. The foliage was still, as though it had never moved. She turned and gazed back at the dead woman.

Still lying in the same position, but something looked different. Then she saw it. The head had tilted to the side, the long hair falling away, and the eyes were now open; and underneath them – like a third eye – the horseshoe pendant was shining in the darkness.

Maya stared. She wanted to run so much, but she found she couldn't move. The pendant went on shining, and something in the dead eyes seemed to shine too. She swallowed. This was madness. She had to break free.

She slipped from behind the oak and crept towards the edge of the thicket. The dusk was now so heavy it was hard to see anything clearly, but somehow she made out the way to go. She stole forward, watching, listening.

Here was the clearing. She remembered stumbling into it on her mad rush here. To the left was the damaged beech tree; to the right the deeper, denser folds of the forest. It was hard to believe she'd crashed through that, yet remembered so little of it.

But that was the way she had to go. She knew that much at least. The path home lay somewhere in that direction. She took a deep breath and set off across the clearing – only to freeze once again.

A second body was lying before her.

Straight ahead.

She made herself creep closer. She had to check this out too. She knew it. She couldn't just run past, however much she wanted to. It was a man this time, and like the woman, clearly dead. She knelt beside him. No movement in the stomach or chest. The eyes were open but they were vacant.

Once again, there was no sign of an injury.

She was trembling now. She forced herself to study the body. The police would ask questions. They'd want a description. She tried to take in what she could, muttering what she saw into the silent air.

'Man about thirty-five, suit, tie, white shirt, red hair . . . '

She stopped, looked again. But there was no mistake. The darkness was draining all colour from the body, yet something red still clung to the hair.

'Red hair,' she went on, 'and . . . and a silver watch.'

Something was moving over to the right, a shadow among the trees at the top of the clearing. She narrowed her eyes and stared; but the shadow was gone and all was gloom again. She tried to stay calm, make herself think.

There were probably lots of paths back to the village but she didn't know them. She had to find the way she'd come, and that meant heading for the trees, whatever else lay in that direction; and she had to go now. She set off across the clearing, walking fast.

She wanted to run. She wanted to burst through the trees and away from this place, but she knew she had to resist. All her instincts told her that the moment she broke into a run, panic would take over. A fast, steady walk was what was needed. Yet even as she walked, she felt a pressure to look back.

She ignored it. She had to scan the trees, watch for danger, find the path, get away. She mustn't look back. Just keep walking, walking, walking. She strode on, step, step, step, but still the pressure grew. She stopped, breathing hard, and turned.

The man's body was still visible, lying on its back, but as with the woman, the head had tilted to the side and the eyes were shining in the darkness. She turned and hurried on towards the trees – only to freeze yet again.

The shadow was back, directly in front of her. The features were hidden, the form blurred, but there was no mistaking the figure standing there, back towards her, bent over a third body, stretched upon the forest floor.

She stared, and as she did so, she saw the figure stiffen, as though it had sensed her, and straighten, and turn towards her. But she saw no more. She was running wild, blundering through thickets, coppices, tawny shrubs.

She had no idea where she was going. All she knew was that she was crashing through branches, brambles, foliage. She heard shouts. Some were hers, some were not. She couldn't catch the words.

They came again, somewhere near. She thought of the shadow and raced on. The shouts continued but she was hardly listening now. All she wanted was to run, run, run. But she didn't know which way to go. Then she saw it. Straight ahead.

She stopped, gasping, and peered into the darkness. Before her was a wall of trees – and something else. Two yellow eyes, watching her;

and now a head, and a body. Then she saw what it was.

A fox.

Recollection came streaming back. She'd seen a fox earlier, perhaps this very one. She remembered it now. It had been on the path and she'd followed it into the forest, leaving Tom behind. But why had she done that? And why had she forgotten about it till now?

'What do you want?' she heard herself say.

The yellow eyes closed, opened, closed again.

And in the space where they had been, she saw a narrow path through the trees.

She tore down it, screaming. But here were the shouts again, and they were closer than ever. She ran on, on, the voices growing louder – and then she fell. She saw leaves, branches, the trunk of a tree, the face of the forest floor as she tumbled upon it.

And a shadow leaning over her.